"I WANT YOU. I INTEND TO HAVE YOU," HE SAID WITH GENTLE MOCKERY.

"I don't play games, Roan," Gem said quietly. "I don't want an affair with you." She shrugged at the disbelief in his eyes. "I didn't say you can't make me want you physically. You know you can. I know it too. But I'm not interested in casual relationships. I won't give in."

"We'll see, honey," he murmured with easy humor. "I've shown you before that what you intend is not what you really want. I'll do it again."

Gem shrugged. Words meant nothing to him. It was her actions that would convince him . . . if anything could. The battle lines were clearly drawn. . . .

A CANDLELIGHT ECSTASY ROMANCE ®

130 CONFLICT OF INTEREST, *Jayne Castle*
131 RUN BEFORE THE WIND, *Joellyn Carroll*
132 THE SILVER FOX, *Bonnie Drake*
133 WITH TIME AND TENDERNESS, *Tira Lacy*
134 PLAYING FOR KEEPS, *Lori Copeland*
135 BY PASSION BOUND, *Emma Bennett*
136 DANGEROUS EMBRACE, *Donna Kimel Vitek*
137 LOVE SONG, *Prudence Martin*
138 WHITE SAND, WILD SEA, *Diana Blayne*
139 RIVER ENCHANTMENT, *Emma Bennett*
140 PORTRAIT OF MY LOVE, *Emily Elliott*
141 LOVING EXILE, *Eleanor Woods*
142 KINDLE THE FIRES, *Tate McKenna*
143 PASSIONATE APPEAL, *Elise Randolph*
144 SURRENDER TO THE NIGHT, *Shirley Hart*
145 CACTUS ROSE, *Margaret Dobson*
146 PASSION AND ILLUSION, *Bonnie Drake*
147 LOVE'S UNVEILING, *Samantha Scott*
148 MOONLIGHT RAPTURE, *Prudence Martin*
149 WITH EVERY LOVING TOUCH, *Nell Kincaid*
150 ONE OF A KIND, *Jo Calloway*
151 PRIME TIME, *Rachel Ryan*
152 AUTUMN FIRES, *Jackie Black*
153 ON WINGS OF MAGIC, *Kay Hooper*
154 A SEASON FOR LOVE, *Heather Graham*
155 LOVING ADVERSARIES, *Eileen Bryan*
156 KISS THE TEARS AWAY, *Anna Hudson*
157 WILDFIRE, *Cathie Linz*
158 DESIRE AND CONQUER, *Diana Dunaway*
159 A FLIGHT OF SPLENDOR, *Joellyn Carroll*
160 FOOL'S PARADISE, *Linda Vail*
161 A DANGEROUS HAVEN, *Shirley Hart*
162 VIDEO VIXEN, *Elaine Raco Chase*
163 BRIAN'S CAPTIVE, *Alexis Hill Jordan*
164 ILLUSIVE LOVER, *Jo Calloway*
165 A PASSIONATE VENTURE, *Julia Howard*
166 NO PROMISE GIVEN, *Donna Kimel Vitek*
167 BENEATH THE WILLOW TREE, *Emma Bennett*
168 CHAMPAGNE FLIGHT, *Prudence Martin*
169 INTERLUDE OF LOVE, *Beverly Sommers*

PROMISES IN THE NIGHT

Jackie Black

A CANDLELIGHT ECSTASY ROMANCE ®

Published by
Dell Publishing Co., Inc.
1 Dag Hammarskjold Plaza
New York, New York 10017

Copyright © 1983 by Jackie Black

All rights reserved. No part of this book may be reproduced or transmitted in any form or by any means, electronic or mechanical, including photocopying, recording, or by any information storage and retrieval system, without the written permission of the Publisher, except where permitted by law.

Dell ® TM 681510, Dell Publishing Co., Inc.

Candlelight Ecstasy Romance®, 1,203,540, is a registered trademark of Dell Publishing Co., Inc., New York, New York.

ISBN: 0-440-17160-1

Printed in the United States of America
First printing—September 1983

To Our Readers:

We have been delighted with your enthusiastic response to Candlelight Ecstasy Romances®, and we thank you for the interest you have shown in this exciting series.

In the upcoming months we will continue to present the distinctive sensuous love stories you have come to expect only from Ecstasy. We look forward to bringing you many more books from your favorite authors and also the very finest work from new authors of contemporary romantic fiction.

As always, we are striving to present the unique, absorbing love stories that you enjoy most—books that are more than ordinary romance.

Your suggestions and comments are always welcome. Please write to us at the address below.

Sincerely,

The Editors
Candlelight Romances
1 Dag Hammarskjold Plaza
New York, New York 10017

CHAPTER ONE

"I'm sorry, sir, but we just can't do it. It's against our policy to extend credit, especially to someone who's not local."

The words barely registered in Gem Reasoner's mind as she climbed out of her disreputable-looking but faithful green pickup camper and made her way past the two men standing talking in front of a service bay at the gas station. She did note out of the corner of her eye that the man who was obviously being denied credit was clean if shabbily dressed and that his kindly face bore a worried expression.

"But you don't understand," the man was saying now. "I have a job waiting for me in Arizona, and if I can't get my truck fixed, I'll lose it. I'll sign anything you want if you'll just . . ."

The rest of the conversation was cut off as Gem entered the ladies' restroom and shut the door behind her. Though she felt a vague sympathy for the plight of the decent-looking man, her thoughts were too filled with her successful homecoming to dwell overlong on someone else's troubles.

She entered one of the restroom stalls to change from her sweat-soaked shirt into a cleaner one, wishing her faithful pickup had air conditioning but remaining firmly loyal to it in spite of its lack of beauty and luxury. She had no more than unfastened the first of the row of buttons, however, when she heard the outer door open, followed by the sound of a woman sobbing and a small frightened voice begging, "Mommy, don't cry. Please don't cry."

Gem frowned as she heard the despair in the mother's reply,

made between racking sobs. "I'm sorry, Billy. It'll be all right. I'll stop in a minute. Don't be scared, honey."

Her soft heart torn by what she was hearing, Gem bit her lip, trying to decide if she should offer to help or stay where she was and thereby perhaps avoid embarrassing the distraught woman. Tears and trouble were very private things, and she knew that in her own case she preferred solitude at such moments, though they had been few and far between in her privileged life.

The small voice spoke up again. "Why are you crying, Mommy? Daddy said we'd be all right now that he's got a job. Daddy's going to take care of us . . . isn't he?" The slight doubt creeping into the solid faith of a small child was hurtful to hear, and the mother's answer was even more so.

"Sure . . . sure he will, Billy. He always has. . . ." But the doubt was there in the mother's voice, too, much as she tried to maintain her confidence for the child's sake, and she burst out weeping once again. Gem decided it was time to offer at least a comforting shoulder, even if there was nothing else she could do for the pair. She thrust open the door of the stall, and in a glance took in the haggard, despairing, tearful face of a youthful-looking woman and the pucker beginning to gather on the small face of her four- or five-year-old son. Both looked at her startled, and Gem smiled at them with warm sympathy.

"I'm sorry," she said in her low, husky singer's voice. "I couldn't help overhearing. I don't want to pry, but if there's any way I can help, I'd like to."

The woman immediately began to try to control her emotions, a withdrawn look coming into her tired blue eyes. It was obvious she wasn't inclined to share her private grief with a stranger. But the small towheaded youngster was less reserved. After a long second of evaluation through rounded, beautifully clear blue eyes, he let go of his mother's hand and moved a step closer to Gem.

"My daddy's truck is sick," he pronounced gravely. "And it's making Mommy cry."

"Billy . . ." The boy's mother started to protest his candor, but after she glanced at Gem embarrassedly, something in Gem's clear gray eyes must have touched her, for she faltered in her admonition to her son and then stared helplessly back at Gem.

Gem gave the woman a reassuring look, then turned back to Billy. "Is that your daddy outside talking to the service station man?" she asked gently, making the connection between the conversation she had overheard and Billy's statement.

The firm little rounded chin bobbed up and down in agreement. "He's the best daddy in the whole world!" he stated stoutly, his look daring her to disagree.

"He certainly looked like a good daddy," Gem agreed. And the man *had* looked kind and decent. She then turned to the mother and asked quietly, "What's the trouble with your truck?"

The woman hesitated, wiping her eyes with a hand that looked as though it was no stranger to hard work. "It . . . it's the clutch," she murmured, still obviously embarrassed at making a stranger privy to her troubles, but gaining confidence in Gem slowly. "It's gone out . . . and . . . and we don't have the money right now to fix it." She said the last rather defiantly, her pride obviously hurt at having to confess such a thing. But when Gem made no comment but encouraged the woman to go on with a look, the woman hesitantly continued. "Bill's been out of work for a while . . . through no fault of his own," she asserted vehemently, "and we were just about at the end of our rope when a cousin offered him work in Arizona. We just had enough money to get there, and now . . ." Her shoulders began to shake with renewed sobs, but the woman bit down hard on her lip to still them, and her gaze was steady and defiant as she looked at Gem.

"I see," Gem said matter-of-factly. "That's rough. Do you mind telling me how much it would take to fix the truck?"

The woman hesitated, but Billy, obviously a boy of intelligence, spoke up again. "I heard the man say a hunnerd and fifty. That's a lot, ain't it?"

"*Isn't* it," Billy's mother corrected him absently, her gaze still defiant. And then she made a strong effort to pull herself together. "It doesn't matter," she said with flat despair in her trembling voice. "We haven't got a penny extra anyway. We couldn't pay it if it were only twenty-five dollars." She turned her back on Gem then and ran the cold water to rinse her face. Gem thought she probably didn't want her husband to know she had been crying.

Gem hesitated momentarily, doing some quick mental arithmetic, and realized that if she provided this family with the money they needed, she wouldn't have enough to finish her own journey to her home in Texas. But she wanted to help. And she could, given the right circumstances.

"Excuse me a moment, will you?" she said to Billy and his mother, and couldn't resist tousling Billy's hair as she passed him on her way out of the restroom. He made an automatic swatting movement with his hand in the way of small boys who resent displays of affection from females, but there was a smile on his face instead of the pucker that had been there when Gem had first seen him.

Once outside, Gem wasted no time in seeking out the service station attendant. Her eyes swept the parking area and noted that the father was now seated in the driver's seat of his pickup truck, his head resting on his hand in an attitude of dejection. The attendant was in the office of the station, and he looked up with a polite expression that quickly turned to one of admiration as Gem entered the area. She wasted no time in getting to the point.

"I want to help that family," she said with quiet determination. "But it will take all of my money to do it. Do you have a club in town that needs a singer so I can earn enough money to make my way home if I give these people what I have?"

The man's homely face creased into an expression of astonishment for a moment, but he was obviously a man used to dealing with the quirks of the traveling public, and his astonishment turned to thoughtfulness within a second or two.

"Well, ma'am, I'm not rightly sure if our club needs a singer. We do have one. It's private. Has to be in this state. No liquor by the drink, you know. I reckon I could call up the manager and see what he says."

"Would you please?" Gem requested with dignity. "And could you hurry? I'm afraid they'll leave before we can find out."

The man was shaking his head even as he reached for the telephone. "They ain't goin' nowhere, ma'am. Not with that clutch." He dialed a number quickly and spoke into the phone for a few moments before he held the receiver out to Gem. "Hank wants to talk to you personally, ma'am. He says he can use someone, but he don't want to take no pig in a poke. Excuse the expression, ma'am. I told him he ain't gonna have no complaint about your looks, but he wants to know if you can sing."

Gem took the receiver from the man and spoke into the phone. "Hello," she said in her distinctive, throaty voice. "I'm Gem Reasoner, and I've been making my living singing for two years. Would you like an audition?"

The manager seemed to appreciate her directness, and they made an appointment for an hour later. After the manager had given her directions to the club, Gem hung up the phone and eyed the attendant as he sat leaning back in his swivel chair, eyeing *her* admiringly and grinning like an overgrown ape.

"I'd like you to begin work on that clutch," Gem informed him in a style she had learned from her mother and which seldom failed to get action. This time, however, it was only partially effective. The man stood up, but his expression was doubtful.

"What if you don't get the job?" he inquired dubiously.

"I'll get the job," Gem replied confidently. "But even if I don't, I have a credit card you can charge the expense to." This last was said with a certain reluctance. The credit card had been given to her by her father over two years ago, when she had started out on what Big Jim Reasoner had termed an expedition into idiocy. She had determined at the time she would never use it, however, and so far she had been able to keep that promise to herself. She had earned every penny of her living expenses, and she didn't intend to break her record now. Indeed, if she hadn't already sent her advance from the record company in Nashville that had bought her songs to her bank in Texas, not liking to carry that kind of money, she would have been saved from even having to use the card as a verification of credit.

As she reached into her shoulder bag for the card, she told the attendant, "Take down the number and ascertain that it's a valid card, but don't use it. I'll be back after I get the job to pay you in cash. I just want to make sure you start work on that clutch as soon as possible so these people can get on their way. I'm sure they can't afford to stay the night at a motel."

The attendant shrugged, took the card and verified it by telephone, then handed it back to her. "I don't understand you, lady," he said admiringly. "But I think you're the nicest thing to walk into this station in a long time."

Gem gave him a dimpled smile. "You don't have to understand," she said gently as she turned toward the door. Then she hesitated and turned back to him. "I'd appreciate it if you wouldn't tell these people the money came from me. They're proud. Just tell them you talked to the owner of the station and he decided to accept their credit, will you?"

The attendant shook his head half in disgust and half in admiration. "And what if they turn out to be honest and send the money when they've got it?" he asked dryly.

Gem shrugged. "I'll leave you my address, and you can send it to me," she said with simple logic.

"And if they turn out to be dishonest?" the attendant inquired.

Gem grinned ruefully. "I think they're honest, but if they're not, I'll chalk it up to experience," she said nonchalantly. "Will you do it my way?"

The attendant gave her a long, appraising male look and nodded. "Honey, I don't think there's many men who *wouldn't* do it your way." And before Gem could even blush at his bluntness, he turned away to call through the door to a mechanic in his shop. "Hey, Slim! You finished with that lube job yet?"

A faint echo revealed that Slim was indeed finished with the lube job.

"Okay," the attendant shouted back. "Get ready to fix a clutch!" Then he turned back to Gem and nodded. "We'll get on it," he promised. And as Gem gave him a smile that dazzled his eyes and started out the door, he spoke warningly. "You be careful out at that club, you hear? Like I said, it's private. We got some men in this town that don't know a lady when they see her."

Gem paused, looking back at him in surprise for a second, then flashed a confident smile. "I'll be careful." She nodded, not bothering to explain that she'd had a lot of practice at handling aggressive men. "And thanks for your help," she added gratefully. "See you later." She walked out the door just as Billy and his mother rounded the corner from the restroom.

"Hey, Billy," she said with friendly airiness as she bent to talk to him at eye level. "Guess what? Your daddy's sick truck is going to get fixed." She glanced up at Billy's mother casually then, noting the glimmer of doubtful hope on the woman's face. "I heard the service station attendant talking to the owner on the telephone," she said quietly. "They've decided to let you pay when you can, I think."

The woman's face was reward enough for Gem's efforts, but Billy took things much more prosaically. "I knew Daddy would fix things," he said with undented confidence. "I told you he was a good daddy."

"You sure did," Gem agreed blithly. "And you were right. You're a lucky boy to have a daddy like that."

Billy nodded gravely, then asked in a solemn manner, "What's your name? And do you have a good daddy too?"

"My name is Gem," Gem answered matter-of-factly. "And yes, I have a good daddy too."

"Jim's a boy's name!" Billy said with a touch of puzzled scorn.

Gem shook her head. "Not the way I spell it," she said. "I spell it the way you spell the word for precious stones . . . jewels," she added as the boy wrinkled his brow over "precious stones." "Like this," Gem explained as she pulled a small pendant on a golden chain out from her neck so that Billy could see. "These are small emeralds and diamonds, and big people call them gems."

Billy eyed the pendant with interest. "Did it cost a lot?" he asked somewhat in awe.

"Billy!" His mother protested his rudeness.

"It's all right," Gem said with a laugh. "No, it didn't cost a lot, Billy," she answered. "But it was given to me with love, and that makes it very precious to me. It's my good luck charm."

Billy nodded approvingly. He knew all about luck charms. "Like my rabbit's foot," he asserted manfully.

"That's right," Gem agreed. "But that's not how I got my name. I'm named after my daddy."

Billy looked puzzled and sceptical again, and Gem explained. "My daddy wanted a boy just like you, Billy, but he got me. He couldn't name me Jim since I was a girl, so he named me Gem like the pretty diamonds and emeralds. It sounds the same, but it's feminine."

She gave up and grinned as she saw that she had lost Billy totally with her involved explanation. "Never mind, Billy. *You* just live up to being named after your father, and I think he'll be as proud of you as you are of him."

"I will," Billy promised with all the confidence of youth.

"I've got to go now," Gem said, unable to resist tousling his hair again, knowing his resistance was purely perfunctory. "Good-bye, Billy." And then she turned to his mother, whose countenance fairly shone with the relief she was feeling at seeing her husband's truck being rolled into the service bay. "Good luck," Gem said to the woman, happy to have been able to help put that look on the woman's face.

"Thank you," the woman murmured, anxious to talk to her husband though she took the time to give Gem a warm smile. "We'll be all right now. I'm sure of it."

"I'm sure of it too," Gem answered confidently. "Good-bye."

"Good-bye," the woman said as she took Billy's hand and moved toward where her husband stood watching the service station attendants start to work on his truck.

" 'Bye, Gem," the boy called as he waved at her with a pudgy hand.

" 'Bye, Billy," Gem called back, and then she went to her pickup and climbed into the seat, grimacing as she remembered she never had changed her shirt. *Oh, well,* she thought happily as she started the engine. *I'll just have to remember to keep downwind of the manager while I audition.* And then as she pulled her green pickup out onto the road she murmured, "Come on, Pedro," and patted the battered dash affectionately. "Let's go earn some money so I can go home to Big Jim a winner all the way."

And as she followed the directions the manager of the private club had given her through the tree-shaded streets of the small town, she was already composing a song about a boy called Billy whose daddy had a sick truck.

CHAPTER TWO

As Gem sat perched on a rickety stool facing her audience her demeanor was as calm and ethereally cool as usual, and her voice was steady, clear, and achingly sweet as she sang one of her favorite folk songs. It was only the uncustomary dampness of her palms as she strummed her guitar in accompaniment that betrayed the uneasiness she was feeling, and that manifestation, of course, was not visible to the audience.

There was no one clear reason for her nervousness. Rather, it was a combination of things, the first of which had been the hand-lettered sign on the inside of the front door of this small private club. It read WHAT YOU SEE HERE, WHAT YOU DO HERE . . . LEAVE IT HERE. Immediately upon reading the words Gem had conjured up visions of illegal, immoral goings-on that couldn't bear the light of day, and the implications had left a bad taste in her mouth. She knew the sign didn't refer to the fact that the club served liquor even though this was a "dry" state, for it was perfectly legal to imbibe in the privacy of one's home or in a private club such as this one. Even the discovery that there was a slot machine in a small room at the back of the club hadn't stilled her uneasiness, though the presence of such a machine was clearly a violation of the law and could have been responsible for the sign she disliked so.

Perhaps the single most forceful cause of her fervent wish to have this evening over and done with was the audience's reaction to her music. This crowd was more the foot-stomping country and western type, and they were growing increasingly restless with her sweet, simple ballads. But she was not at all sure it would be wise to introduce more spirited songs into her repertoire, though she knew plenty of them, because she wondered if, once excited, this group of rugged, leering, overwhelmingly male patrons could be controlled.

Well, she was halfway through her program, she consoled herself with dogged determination, and once she was through and had her pay in hand, she could get back on the road to Texas.

Her smoky gray eyes skimmed rapidly over the mostly male faces peering up at her and noted their bold stares, their speculative assessments of her attributes as a woman, and the fact that they seemed to be increasingly aware of her as a woman rather than a performer. There was only one man in the whole place whose expression denoted more boredom than lasciviousness. But his hard face, while sophisticated and by far the most attractive of the lot, held out no hope that he would be sympathetic should Gem's audience decide to turn to more amusing entertainment than listening to her sing, if they were, in fact, listening to her at all.

Gem finished the song she was singing and rather desperately decided to opt for audience participation in the next one in the hope that if they were involved in singing a harmless ballad, they might cease their intent staring, which was beginning to make her skin crawl.

As the last note died away and a smattering of applause greeted the finish of the song, Gem raised her head, tossed back the length of shimmering black hair that had fallen over her shoulder, and faced her audience with a slight smile curving the pale pink of her lips.

"I'm going to need your help on the next one, ladies and gentlemen," she said in her quiet but carrying Texas drawl, which held a hint of tantalizing huskiness in it. "I'll go through the lyrics once, and then, if you will, I'd like you to join me on the chorus the second time through." She raised the dark wings of her patrician eyebrows invitingly and strummed the opening chord on her guitar, then swung into the song in a clear, lilting, spirited voice that caused chills to go down the spines of the more sensitive ones in the group.

The man she had thought the most attractive member of the group let a slight smile curve his firm, beautifully formed lips into a cynical twist. She had been right about his sophistication, but if she had known it, there was a great deal more to him than mere surface sophistication. He was an expert at reading situations and people. He had had to be in order to build up the small oil leasing firm his father had left him into one of the biggest of its kind in the world. And right now he had sized up what was going on in this room, and even in the mind of the slender, somehow elegant-looking performer perched in front of it. He was admiring her for trying to defuse the situation, though he had very little admiration for the female sex in general, and he was attracted to her in a lazy, sexual, half-attentive fashion that would have alarmed Gem unreasonably if she had known what could happen should his attention become fully involved. He had an unbroken record of seduction he himself never gave much thought to, except for a vague appreciation of the fact that whenever he wanted a woman, there always seemed to be one available . . . whether she had planned to be or not.

Tonight, however, Roan Christianson had other things on his mind. He normally wouldn't have been patronizing such a place at all except for the fact that one of the men in the audience, a man who had property Roan wanted to tie up in a lease very badly, had invited him. And Roan was nothing if not persistent. He would dog the man's footsteps to hell and back if it would get him what he wanted.

Gem felt better as the audience joined in on the chorus as she had requested. True, they weren't enthusiastic about it, but they *were* singing, and she hoped their participation would take their minds off more dangerous topics. Consequently she stretched out the song for as long as she could safely do, until she sensed it was time to give them some relief before they stopped of their own accord.

Thinking she was entitled to a short break herself, Gem announced the fact, set her guitar aside, and descended from the podium, taking care not to make eye contact with anyone as she did so. She was dying for a soft drink, and as she passed a harried waitress on the way to the ladies' room, Gem whispered her order to the girl, then continued on her way. Once in the small confines of the only room the club boasted that could be used as a dressing room, Gem sagged against the closed door behind her back and let her muscles relax.

"God!" she whispered softly to herself. "Why didn't I keep more of the money the record company gave me? It was idiotic to send almost all of it to the bank when I could just as easily have kept aside enough for an emergency!"

But, then, this was the first emergency she'd had in the entire two years she had been traveling the country performing to earn her expenses, while the geography and people of the land inspired the songs she wrote. And at last she had managed to sell the majority of those songs to a record company in Nashville. Now she could go home again, and not as a failure, either! That fact brightened the opalescent light in her gray eyes to a shine of quiet satisfaction and curved her lovely mouth into a smile of anticipation.

Her father, Big Jim Reasoner, admired initiative, drive, and ambition in anyone, but most of all he admired success. And since he had an easier time attributing such qualities to a male than to a female . . . and since he had been adamantly opposed to her choice of careers and especially to her recent two-year odyssey, Gem was looking forward to laying her accomplishments before him with almost as much pleasure as she'd derived from the accomplishments themselves. She had come through her journey unscathed, so far, and with proof that it had not been a foolish escapade, as her father had termed it, in the form of a contract with a national recording company—all contrary to the dire predictions of her sire, and all certain to cause her somewhat snobbish mother pained embarrassment. Gem could hardly wait!

But right now she had to finish this one last night on the road, and she had to do it without any unpleasantness to spoil her good record. Remembering that fact, Gem frowned, straightened her shoulders, and crossed to the small sink to wash her hands. As she dried them she gazed at her reflection in the mirror almost with disinterest, checking automatically to see that her makeup didn't need refreshening or her hair combing.

Her eyes fastened on to the small pendant around her neck, and she smiled, then touched the circlet for good luck. It might be inexpensive, but it had been bought by the sweat of Pedro's brow and given to her out of pure affection, and the sight of it never failed to lift her spirits.

Gem took a deep breath, straightened the waistband of her full-length, flowing, flower-bedotted culottes, touched the one strap over her left shoulder of the simple white top she wore, then turned, prepared to face again the onslaught of male eyes that on this particular night had managed to unnerve her. She was not shy, and she was used to audiences, but this one . . . well, she would be more than glad when the evening was over.

Emerging from the room, Gem unconsciously settled the classic lines of her face into a look of calm composure. She approached the main room in a slow, dignified walk, refusing to give in to the frown threatening to crease her smooth brow at the increased decibel level that had become so noticeable since her short break. The waitress caught sight of her as Gem paused in the entranceway and hurried over to bring her her drink, acting as though it were a decided imposition to have to provide one to someone who wouldn't be expected to give her a tip. Gem's full lower lip twitched slightly at the girl's attitude. She was thinking what mincemeat her mother would have made of such service, and indeed, if Gem had felt it worth the trouble, she could have done the same. But it was not, and after a barely murmured "Thank you" she took the drink into her delicate hand and raised it to her mouth to take a long swallow to ease her dry throat. She was lowering the glass when she felt the clasp of a huge clammy hand on her bare shoulder.

"Well, hello, sweetheart," a slurred, drunken voice said gratingly in her ear. "Waitin' for me, are ya?"

Gem had immediately tensed at the unwelcome touch, and now she turned a pair of glacial eyes on the man. Her icy voice signaled her distaste when she replied, though she did so quietly.

"No. Will you take your hand away, please?"

The man's heavy-jowled ruddy face went a deeper shade of red, and his bloodshot piggish eyes narrowed threateningly. "Don't try to play the high-toned lady with me, girlie," he sneered. "You wouldn't be here if you was a real lady."

"I am here to sing," Gem replied coldly as she shrugged her shoulder disdainfully to dislodge the man's grip. "And that is *all* I'm here for."

A nasty smile twisted the man's rubbery lips as he imprisoned her wrist in a grip of steel. "Maybe you don't know who I am, girlie?" he said in a bragging tone that disgusted Gem.

But she sensed an innate brutality in the man that frightened her as well, though she was certain it would be a mistake to show her fear to this bully. She turned her profile to him to scan the room with her eyes, searching for the manager of the club. "I don't particularly care who you are," she said with a slightly bored, admirable composure. "But I do care about who touches me, and I'm not fond of bruises, so I repeat, will you please let me go."

She tried to couch the request as an order in the style she had learned from her mother. But she was relieved when she finally caught the eye of the manager, and she shot him a look that was unmistakably an appeal for help. The manager frowned at seeing who held her, then chewed his lip hesitantly, his reluctance to come to her rescue apparent.

Gem suppressed a groan of dismay at that reluctance even as the man beside her lurched closer and wrapped a heavy arm around her shoulders.

"Now listen here, sweet thing," he grated at her, wafting his liquor-tainted breath over her face as he did so. "You be nice to me, and I'll be nice to you . . . get it?"

Gem controlled a visible shudder as she took his meaning. Obviously the man regarded her as little better than a prostitute, and he was offering to pay for her services, not realizing that money was the last thing likely to make her view his proposal with favor. Indeed, she couldn't think of anything on God's green earth that *would* make her amenable to what this man had in mind.

As she searched the room desperately with her eyes for any help she could find, since the manager, if he intended to help at all, was taking his time about it, Gem's gaze suddenly collided with a pair of tawny-brown gold-flecked orbs that seemed simultaneously aware of and disdainful of her plight. But as Gem's eyes clung to his the man she had designated earlier as both attractive and sophisticated frowned slightly, then compressed his full, sensuous mouth into a line of impatience, but even as he did so he was getting to his feet and starting in her direction.

Gem held her breath, willing the man to bring all six feet of his tautly muscled, well-shaped body to her rescue. She remained silent as her pursuer continued to breathe what he considered inducements into her ear, determined she was *not* going to parry his disgusting suggestions, nor was she going to gag as his foul breath wafted over her. She hoped her cold attitude and her silence would give the animal his answer more effectively than words could.

Her would-be rescuer came up to Gem, his stance relaxed and easy, his brown eyes alert and humorous as he flicked his gaze over her, then her unwelcome companion. "Well, darlin'," he drawled familiarly, "is our date still on tonight when you get through here?"

Startled for a moment by his opening remark, Gem nevertheless played along. "Of course, it is," she tossed back flirtatiously. "In fact, I'm looking forward to it so much, I'm thinking of cutting my program short."

The slight touch of grimness in her tone told her rescuer all he needed to know about her real meaning, but he gave no sign that she had meant other than what she'd said. He smiled down at her, a warm glow in his dark eyes rewarding her for her quick uptake on his ploy. Then those eyes shifted to the man on her right, the warmth quickly turning to a lazy challenge. "Hello, Rawlins. Not trying to beat my time with the lady here, are you?"

Perhaps if the man had been less inebriated, he would have backed down immediately, as it was clear from his expression that he accorded Gem's rescuer the respect Gem was already convinced this stranger deserved. But it seemed Rawlins was going to put up at least a token resistance to maintain his pride.

"Huh! What do you mean *lady*?" he sneered, giving Gem a contemptuous look, then his contester for her favors a man-to-man smirk. "You ain't gonna tell me *you* want her, are you, Christianson? You can afford better."

Even through her anger at Rawlins's insult Gem watched fascinated as the man Rawlins had referred to as Christianson all at once seemed to grow taller, though she was sure he had merely straightened his shoulders. Perhaps it was the look of dangerous alertness that had come over his rugged, somewhat ruthless face that made him appear even more formidable than he had at first seemed to be.

"I never did think much of your taste, Rawlins," he replied on a hard note. "I think if you'll look a little closer, you'll realize *you* can't afford this sort of quality."

Both Gem and her pursuer flushed at that, if for very different reasons. Gem, unused to having herself discussed as though she were a piece of merchandise to be haggled over, even if this Christianson did afford her the distinction of being "quality" goods, was incensed at the position she found herself in. And Rawlins was equally insulted at being labeled unable to afford something.

"If you had half the business sense you think you do," he now sneered at Christianson, "I could afford anything I wanted."

"That's a matter of opinion, isn't it?" Christianson tossed back at him, his tone cold and hard. "And until our little business deal is settled, we won't know who has better sense, will we?" He smiled a mirthless smile at the fuming Rawlins. "Meanwhile, I don't take kindly to having what's mine mauled and insulted by anyone. Let the lady go, Rawlins."

It was not so much a challenge as it was an order, and the man Gem knew only as Christianson gave it with such flinty assurance that Gem was not surprised when the red-faced Rawlins obeyed. She was unable to suppress a shudder at being released from the loathsome Rawlins's embrace, nor was she able to conceal her gratitude from her rescuer. Her smoky gray eyes were eloquent with emotion as she quickly stepped away from Rawlins and instinctively moved to stand within the shelter of Christianson's arm. He took her into that shelter without a second's hesitation, so that Gem was pressed against the warmth of his side and felt the strength of his long-fingered hand on her bare arm. Her flesh quivered at the contact, but she was hardly aware of the sensation, engrossed as she was in waiting for the repulsive Rawlins to react to his comeuppance.

The portly Rawlins stood glaring at the two of them for a long moment while Gem gazed coldly back at him and Christianson merely faced him down with unmoving calculation. Then Rawlins obviously came to his senses about where his interests lay because he forced a wavery smile onto his mouth and then laughed heartily. "You're right." He unbent with awkward submission to Christianson. "I don't want to be poaching on what belongs to another man," he said insultingly, causing Gem to stiffen where she stood. "I'll see you tomorrow, Christianson." Rawlins spoke as though nothing had happened to put the two men at odds. "When we're both sober, we'll get our business done."

Gem thought that a face-saving statement since as far as she could see, Christianson was not even close to being drunk. But her rescuer merely smiled a tight-lipped smile and tipped his mane of reddish brown hair in a nod to the other man, whereupon Rawlins saluted him with a one-fingered wave and moved away. But something about the ugly look in his cold piggish eyes told Gem it would be as well for anyone to stay out of his way for the time being, as he looked the type who wouldn't flinch at stabbing an adversary in the back.

With Rawlins out of the way at last Gem quickly stepped away from her rescuer. "Thank you," she got out on a soft, quick breath. "But be careful of him." She nodded her head at the retreating Rawlins. "He's a snake in the grass if I ever saw one."

She had half-turned to go back to the podium and keep her bargain to provide the evening's entertainment when she felt the warmth of Christianson's hand on her wrist. She stopped, torn between wanting to be gracious to the man she owed her rescue to and hoping she hadn't stepped from the frying pan into the fire. "Yes?" she asked with cautious stiffness.

"I'll stick around until you're finished to make sure you get away safely," Christianson said, a smiling quirk to his firm, sensuous mouth, a look of amusement in his tawny eyes. "You're right about Rawlins. If he sees you leave alone, he'll be after you."

Gem bit her lip, then conceded that Christianson might be right. "Thank you, Mr. Christianson," she said with stiff primness. "You'll only have to walk me to my truck. I'll be all right after that."

"The name is Roan," her rescuer drawled. "And I wouldn't be too sure about being all right. 'Snake in the grass' is a mild way of describing that one's character."

Gem frowned, uncertain and fearful at Roan's words; then she simply shrugged and made her way back to the podium, unconsciously rubbing her wrist as she went, uncertain whether she wanted to wipe Roan Christianson's touch away or savor the lingering warmth of it. She would have been even more uncertain and fearful if she could have seen the light of awakened interest in Roan Christianson's darkly appreciative gaze as he watched her move gracefully back to the podium to resume singing, or known the tenor of his thoughts. He was thinking that his night in this one-horse town held possibilities he would have sworn were nonexistent a few short moments ago. And then with characteristic single-mindedness he returned to his table to begin again his pursuit of the lease which was his only reason for being here.

CHAPTER THREE

Gem stood with barely concealed impatience as the manager counted out her earnings into her outstretched hand.

"Thank you," she drawled wryly as she stuffed the bills into her purse and slung her guitar strap over her shoulder. She had left the case in the pickup as she found it easier to carry the instrument this way than to lift the weight of the case and the guitar combined. Her eyes were cool as she took her leave of her erstwhile employer, expressing clearly her contempt for his failure to come to her aid earlier in the evening. The man looked uncomfortable for a moment, but then he shrugged his shoulders as if to say *What the hell, you can't win them all* before he turned away to begin the process of closing the club for the night.

Gem strode rapidly to the door leading outside, her gaze raking the sign she disliked so much with displeasure. She was pushing the door open when Roan Christianson loomed up beside her, his downward gaze showing amusement at her startlement at seeing him. She had decided he had forgotten about his promise to see her safely away from the club and had been torn between a shrugging acceptance of the fact and an unwelcome twinge of regret that she wouldn't be seeing him again. That alone made her somewhat wary of the man. There was no point in becoming attracted to him, as she was sure she would never see him again after tonight.

"You thought I'd forgotten," he stated with certainty, his amusement more pronounced. "If you knew me better, you'd know I never forget anything."

Gem shrugged, uneasily disturbed by his words. She had been around men like him all her life—her own father had a large share of the masterful self-assurance this man bore so easily—but somehow Roan Christianson's statement that he never forgot anything made her wonder if he weren't the type to bear a grudge once offended, a trait her father did not share.

"I would have understood if you had," she said more calmly than she felt. "After all, you don't know me. There's no reason why you should protect me."

Roan Christianson pushed the door open for her as he laughed easily. "Honey, in this part of the country a man's a heel if he doesn't come to the aid of a lady in distress," he said with mocking gallantry. "We're not all like Rawlins."

Gem couldn't suppress a shudder at the mention of the man's name. "Thank God!" she uttered forcefully. "He made my skin crawl."

Speaking the words recalled to her how Roan's touch had affected her, and she wished she hadn't said anything when he laughed softly again and said, "Yes, I could see that. And I thought it was a pure shame to see something so fine degraded by a pig like that."

His tone was silkily caressing, and for an instant Gem felt as though his voice had touched her every bit as disturbingly as his hands had earlier. Determined to ignore the sensation, she kept her tone brisk as she replied, "I appreciate what you did, and thank you for being here to walk me to my truck. I suppose Rawlins is gone now, but I'm glad to know I don't have to make that walk alone in the dark."

"Don't be too sure he's gone," Roan Christianson said softly, indicating with his head the shape of a dark car parked off to the side. "Rawlins isn't a man to leave loose ends when his interest is aroused."

Startled into a momentary pause by the information, Gem felt Roan's hand at her back keeping her moving. "Don't worry about it," he drawled. "I'm here."

Gem shot a sideways look up at his profile and was instantly reassured by the strength she saw there. "I can't wait to get on the road to Texas," she said with heartfelt sincerity. "I should be able to make it halfway home before I stop for the night."

She felt an arrested stillness in Roan's strong arm at her back for an instant, but then it was gone, and she thought she must have imagined the sensation. "You don't mind dropping me off at my motel, do you?" he said with a casual lack of emphasis. "I came out here with someone else, and they've already left. They had to get home, but I wanted to keep my promise to you."

What could she say? The man had gone out of his way to help her twice now, and Gem couldn't leave him without transportation, though it was on the tip of her tongue to suggest he ride with the loathsome Rawlins. But that would have been entirely too lacking in gratitude, and where was the harm in giving him a lift, anyway? "I'll be glad to," she said quietly but not entirely truthfully. She sensed a danger in this man she couldn't pinpoint and was impatient with herself for her uncustomary reaction to him. Surely she could stand five minutes in the company of a man who attracted her, even if it wasn't going to lead anywhere? She must simply be on edge because of the experiences of the night.

When they came to her dilapidated pickup camper, she searched in her bag for the key, then unlocked and opened the driver's door as Roan went around to the other side. When she had leaned over to open his door, he climbed into the seat, looking amused once again at her mode of transportation. He glanced into the back at the bunk where she sometimes slept and at the jumble of possessions she had accumulated in her travels, and grinned. "How convenient," he drawled, and then at Gem's cold look he added, "I imagine it saves you traveling expenses to have your own bed," and his tone and look were so innocently bland, Gem relaxed, thinking she had read more into his opening statement than he had meant.

"Yes, it does," she asserted with some asperity. "I've been traveling for two years, and there have been some lean times, though not many. At any rate, I'm on my way home now, so I won't have to sleep with Pedro again for a long time."

It was her turn to grin at Roan's startled, speculative look. "Pedro is my truck's name," she said mockingly, patting the dash before starting the engine with a roar. "I named him after my best friend."

She ignored the look on Roan's face, which showed clearly that he was now speculating about just how close a friend this Pedro was. "Which way to your motel?" she asked crisply, then followed his directions carefully as he gave them with cool precision.

Gem noted in her rearview mirror that the car which had been parked at the club started up and stayed on her tail as she made her way to Roan's motel, but the fact, other than causing her to experience a cold anger at the persistent Rawlins, didn't unduly alarm her until she drew up before the door to Roan's room. Rawlins's car drew up a few yards away and stopped.

"He isn't giving up, is he?" Roan drawled on a hard note. "I wouldn't put it past him to follow you and force you off the road if you drive off alone."

Gem swung anxious gray eyes toward her passenger. "Should we call the police?" she asked uncertainly.

Roan's gold-flecked eyes swept over her in a remote look. He hesitated for a moment, then spoke slowly. "Ordinarily I'd speak to him myself. But I want to do business with him, and there won't be much chance of that if we call the police and embarrass him or if I push him much further than I already have. He's a prominent man in town, too, and there's always the chance the police would be more inclined to take his side than ours."

Gem compressed her soft mouth in frustration, banging her small fist on the steering wheel. "Damn the man," she muttered under her breath. "I hate him already, and I don't even know him!"

"Your instincts are good," Roan smiled faintly, "but the fact of the matter is, hating him won't get us out of this predicament."

Gem flashed him an angry glance, then softened it into one of frustration. "What do you suggest?" she asked dryly. "We can't sit here all night." She was about to throw caution to the winds and take her chances on the road when Roan made a suggestion that, even though it made sense, made her tense with apprehension.

"We could always go into my room for a while," he said with a careful lack of aggressiveness. "Once Rawlins becomes convinced we plan to stay together, he may decide to leave us in peace."

Gem stiffened, hesitating about how to respond to his suggestion. She was shocked to find it as appealing as she did. Good heavens! she thought resentfully, eyeing the male body beside her in a lightning assessment that only increased her dilemma. She wasn't *used* to reacting to a man like this! And it wasn't from lack of opportunity, either. She had been turning down propositions from men for so long, she normally did it without hesitation. But Roan Christianson wasn't behaving as though he even had a proposition in mind, and she was reacting as though she *wanted* him to!

"I . . . er . . . don't . . ." she stumbled. Roan's easy laugh stopped her short.

"Come on, honey," he teased mockingly. "I meant it when I called you a lady. You aren't going to have to fight for your virtue with me."

His teasing warmth relaxed her even as it left her with a curious sense of disappointment. If she had known the extent of Roan Christianson's experience with women, she would not have felt even remotely relaxed. And certainly not if she had known about the pleased, complacent self-satisfaction he was experiencing now as he saw that ill-advised relaxation.

"Well," she said reluctantly, "I suppose . . ." Then with an angry shrug of her shoulders she capitulated. "All right, Mr. Christianson. I only hope this doesn't take long. I'm already tired, and I want to put a lot of miles behind me before I sleep tonight!"

Roan hid his satisfaction, merely gazing at her with lazy reproach as he teased her again. "If we're going to share a motel room—however briefly—don't you think you could call me Roan instead of Mr. Christianson?" Then he laughed outright as he saw Gem's reluctant answering smile. "Come on," he said through his laughter as he opened his door. "Let's give Rawlins something to think about."

Gem carefully locked the door behind him before she climbed out her side and locked that door too. Having a man like Rawlins stalking her made her even more cautious than she was normally. When she came around to the front of the truck, she was a little disconcerted and subsequently breathless when Roan clasped her to his side, then lowered his head to give her a brief warming kiss on her mouth. "Play the part," he whispered softly, his brown eyes gleaming with amusement at her wide-eyed surprise when he raised his head. "This is for Rawlins's benefit, remember? You'll have to forget you're a lady for a little while."

Gem looked at him doubtfully for a second before her humor was able to reassert itself in the face of her startling reaction to Roan's kiss. She felt branded by it, but she mustn't let him know that. The situation they were walking into was dangerous enough as it was. "All right," she whispered back impishly as she wrapped her arm around his back, almost withdrawing it when she felt the heat of his muscles against her hand. He felt altogether too good for her to be unaffected, but she knew she had to appear to be so. "Is this all right?" She managed to sound amused, though the effort cost her.

"Ummm . . . it could be better, but it'll do," he answered consideringly as he withdrew his motel room key from his pocket and inserted it in the lock.

Gem was a little offended at his statement, but she kept a smile on her lips and an unperturbed look in her eyes as Roan ushered her into his room. It was tastefully decorated in blues and greens, but all Gem could focus on was the single bed in the center of it. She felt her breath quickening as she heard the door closing firmly behind her, and she made herself walk a few steps inside, then turn casually to look at Roan. He was shrugging out of his suit jacket, and Gem swallowed as she saw the muscles in his arms and shoulders moving with the exertion. Somehow he looked even more attractive in his white shirt than he had in the chocolate brown of the suit, and when he began to loosen his tie, Gem had to swallow again and avert her eyes to keep from showing how he affected her.

"What shall we do to pass the time?" she asked with bright cheerfulness as she tossed her handbag onto the bed and sauntered casually toward the television set. The quality of Roan's stillness made her swing around to face him, and her breath caught in her throat at the lazy look of sensuality on his handsome face.

"Honey, that's a loaded question in this situation," he drawled caressingly. "I'm trying to be a gentleman, but it's getting harder all the time." Then he smiled charmingly at her to erase the tense wariness he saw in her face. "Why don't you turn on the television, and we'll just have to hope we don't get an X-rated movie."

Gem's response to his suggestive humor was a low, husky laugh that surprised her with its hint of invitation. And as she turned away to fumble with the few channels this small town boasted, she was even more surprised to find that she was actually feeling pleased and excited at Roan's show of interest in her as a woman. It was as though in stepping through that motel room door into this very private, very intimate setting, she had shed a whole layer of lifelong inhibitions to don the skin of a sensual woman ready for . . . whatever might happen.

The only clear channel on the TV set provided a movie that, while it wasn't X-rated, came very close to being R-rated. The scene at the moment was of a couple of well-known actors lying on a bed participating in a sensuous kiss that brought prickles of awareness to Gem's spine. She heard Roan's low chuckle an instant before she felt the warmth of his hands on her shoulders.

"You're not having any luck at all tonight, are you, honey?" he murmured with gentle amusement as he ran his hands softly down the sides of her bare arms, causing Gem first to tense, then to melt at his touch. "I wish you weren't a lady," he added, whispering sensuously into her ear, his breath disturbing the fine tendrils of dark hair in a feather-soft movement that was a caress in itself.

"Wh-why?" Gem quavered on a disturbed note, thinking that if she were going to back away from this unexpected, captivating adventure, now was the time to do it. But she didn't. Instead she stayed where she was, straining for more of Roan Christianson's touch instinctively.

"You know why," Roan breathed softly, pulling her backward against him so imperceptibly that Gem was barely aware he'd done so. "You're beautiful, you feel delicious, and I'm only a man. There's a very fine line between a gentleman and the man beneath, darlin', and I'm finding it harder and harder to make the distinction." The low-timbred seductiveness of his voice as he muttered the words against her cheek, then feathered his lips down to the curve of her softly rounded jawline and back up to her ear, where he traced a delicate line with his tongue, brought a shiver of delicious reaction to Gem's slender frame.

"Roan . . ." She almost groaned his name, then willingly went silent as he reached a hand to her chin and turned her face toward him, gently enveloping her parted lips with his mouth. Without using force he coaxed, explored, and stroked enticingly with his tongue until Gem found herself turning in his arms to wrap her arms around his neck while he gathered her body to his, still without exerting the considerable strength she felt in him.

Gem leaned into him, offering the secrets of her mouth as she never had before, totally caught up in this fascinating onslaught on her senses as the rest of the world fell dizzily away. Roan took her offering with all the skill of his experience, careful not to disturb her by demanding too much too soon. While he cooperated with and built upon Gem's response, he let her set the pace, enjoying to the full the moment when she became impatient with his restraint and began to enter into their lovemaking more aggressively.

Her tongue sought his, tentatively at first, then with more assurance as Roan's engaged it in a restrained duel, enticing her to explore more deeply, then taking the initiative to thrust with his. While their mouths clung, sipped, tasted erotically, Roan's hands moved from her shoulders to mold her pliant body against his, stroking as they traveled to her hips and pulled them more securely against his. The heat she felt there intoxicated her while at the same time it gave a very distant warning of the irreversible path she was on.

Breaking away briefly from the domination of Roan's mouth, Gem raised slumberously passionate, darkly gray eyes to his lazy, sensual brown ones. "Roan . . ." she half-questioned weakly. "I . . . I didn't intend . . ."

Roan's look silenced her with its gentle possessiveness. "I know, baby," he answered softly, maintaining her trust. "But you won't be sorry your good intentions went astray. I'm going to show you what happens when you get what you want instead of what you intended."

Gem almost whimpered when Roan took her mouth again, her own opening greedily for his taste, as though it had a mind of its own. Taking advantage of that greed, Roan stepped up the pace of his seduction, becoming more dominant, more forceful with his kisses, more bold in his caresses. Gem barely felt the tug on the zipper of her white top, and she didn't care that Roan had bared her breasts to his touch. He didn't give her time to care, as he followed the downward slipping of the garment with his mouth on the heated, rounded globe that became visible to his eyes and his touch.

"Ah . . ." Gem's gasp of pleasure came thickly from her throat as Roan tugged gently on the nipple with his lips, then stroked the tautness with his tongue and gently suckled the softness he drew into his mouth.

He lifted her into his arms and deposited her on the bed, following her down until they lay side by side, his head buried at her breast, and Gem's hands cradling it to keep it there. She was mindless in her pleasure, her seduction complete before

Roan had her fully stripped and lying nude in his arms for his complete delectation. He led her patiently to the point where she felt bold enough to do anything he wanted, even to obeying his soft huskily worded demand that she help him undress.

Gem's hands were shaking with her need as she unfastened the buttons to his shirt. When it was off, she ran her fingers through the thick mat of hair on his chest, savoring tactilely the hard muscles, the heated skin, the sheer maleness of him. He let her explore for long moments before he guided her hands to his belt, then released them to let her fumble with the buckle on her own as he returned his attention to her breasts, an area he had already found to be particularly vulnerable to his caresses.

As Gem finished undressing him she sensed his control was weakening, and the feeling of power and pleasure this gave her was nothing short of intoxicating. It released a heretofore unknown wantonness in her nature that would have shocked her a mere hour earlier but which now seemed entirely natural. She began to provoke him with delicious premeditation, using tactics she hadn't even been aware she'd known until Roan retaliated in the way she had meant for him to all along without realizing what it was she wanted.

His patient gentleness fell away with startling abruptness to be replaced by such dominating, powerful passion that Gem felt swept out of reality entirely, her only thought to respond to the demands Roan made, to please him, to be pleasured in her turn, to grasp for the ecstasy he promised but still withheld with perverse strength of will.

Finally she could stand it no more. She begged for what she wanted with sobbing helplessness, only then discovering that that was what Roan had been waiting for. "Please . . . oh, God, please, Roan!" Gem moaned her plea. "I want all of you! I want it now! Don't make me wait any longer!"

She was held by the fierce light of satisfied male arousal that blazed from Roan's tawny eyes as he moved over her to give her what she was pleading for. "I only needed you to ask, baby," he growled on a note that was almost savage with his own need. "Now you can have it all."

His thrust, for all its power, for all its devastating passion, was not rough, nor did it hurt, for all Gem's inexperience. She met it as though she *were* experienced, guided by some instinct Roan had awakened and exploited to its fullest. In a sense this was as though it were the first time for her. Her first, fumbling teenaged attempts at lovemaking had hardly been worthy of the name. Indeed, it had been so disappointing, she had never wanted to try it again . . . not until now . . . not until Roan Christianson had shown her the difference between inexperienced groping and full-fledged passion.

He made her joyous expression of that passion complete to the last instant, leading her, being led by her, until together they gained the peak of ecstasy Gem strained for with all her heart and soul and mind, knowing the gift would set the seal on this most fascinating, engrossing, wondrous adventure into a world she had never known before and which held out the promise of being the best there was to be had.

She cried out her pleasure at the last, her voice drowned in Roan's hoarse echo of that cry, and then she let the contentment and relaxation come, slowly, achingly, a tender pleasure all its own.

They lay tangled together, each savoring in his and her own way the memory of what they'd had together and the exhausted, poignant sadness that it was now over. Gem felt drained of all energy, empty, yet somehow complete. Her eyes remained closed as she felt sleep coming to claim her, a soft smile welcoming the gentle darkness. She clung to Roan as he moved off her, cradling her head in the hollow of his shoulder, unwilling to go alone into the land of oblivion, needing his arms around her on the journey.

Roan obliged, his full, sensuous mouth curved into a smile of contented satisfaction as he enfolded Gem's pliant body against him, not even wondering why he didn't feel the need to disengage himself immediately, as he invariably did when he'd had what he wanted from a woman. The closest he came to acknowledging

Gem's difference was a vague thought that she still needed his protection, and the payment she gave for that protection was well worth the effort. And then he, too, dropped into oblivion, sleeping more soundly than he had ever found possible before in a strange bed with a woman he had never set eyes on until this most gratifying night.

CHAPTER FOUR

Twice more during the night Roan claimed her, each time with more familiarity, more demand for her participation. Gem responded as though Roan had every right to make those demands, her mind at first groggy with sleep, then beset with passion that precluded clear thought. It was as though she had changed within the space of hours from a totally independent woman to a wife, or more accurately, a mistress, used to this man's claim upon her, and, indeed, more than happy to be subject to that claim.

Toward dawn Gem fell into a deep, exhausted sleep that Roan left undisturbed as he napped himself, then rose to shower and dress and pack his things. His state of mind struck him as peculiar as he prepared, as he had many times in the past, to leave a woman who had pleasured him. He found that when his glance fell upon Gem where she lay sleeping like an exhausted child, her raven hair spread around her classically beautiful face and contrasting sharply with the white of the pillow case, one small hand curled against her cheek, he experienced an instant surge of conflicting emotions. One part of him wanted to join her in bed again and experience the delightful contrast of unbridled passion shining from the coolness of wide gray eyes and pouting sensuality on the innocent sweetness of her mouth. The other part of him wanted to protect her from hurt, either physical or emotional, and that surprised him, since she was the first woman he had ever considered in need of protection.

His strongly chiseled lips bore a frown in reaction to his

unusual reactions to this woman, but he fought down the sensations she engendered in him. Having never considered women particularly important in his life before, he was uncomfortable with the feeling Gem evoked and was impatient to have done with it.

Still, as he prepared to leave the room and glanced at her once again, he felt she deserved something for the pleasure she had given, and as he was a man who always paid his debts, he hesitated, then crossed the room to fish in the drawer of the dresser for paper and pen. He penned a note in his bold, clear handwriting, threw the pen down, and recrossed the room to the door to grasp his bag and slip out into the morning sunshine.

His stride was long and quick as he made his way to the restaurant adjoining the motel, his frown denoting his sense of having left something undone. By the time he'd finished a light breakfast, his frown had degenerated into a scowl that quickly discouraged his flirtatious waitress from any further attempts to engage his interest.

As he came outside into the fresh air and sunshine again, his glance fell upon a shop across the street—a jeweler's—which was just opening for business, and his expression turned to thoughtful speculation. He stood thinking for a moment and then relaxed, a curious smile erasing the harshness from his rugged features. Then he crossed the street to enter the shop.

Inside, an elderly woman clerk looked up at him in surprise as he made a quick tour of the showcases. It took him less than three minutes to spot what he wanted, and with an imperious gesture of his forefinger he pointed out to the clerk the pair of earrings he had in mind.

The clerk fluttered to attention at the sight of the price tag attached to the baubles, and her manner was both deferential and eager as she brought them out for his inspection. A wry smile flickered over Roan's features as he nodded his head that he would take them.

"Your wife will love these, I'm sure," the woman twittered as she began to fill out the sales slip. "Diamonds and emeralds are always a sure way to a woman's heart, and these are exceptionally good." When she didn't receive an answer, the woman hastily bent her head to the sales slip again. "Will you be paying by check or credit card?" she asked.

"Cash," was Roan's one-word answer, delivered in a sardonic tone.

The woman blinked at that, her expression dubious and a little in awe of a man who could afford to carry that kind of money around with him. She named the total after adding tax and watched wide-eyed as Roan reached into his thick wallet and extracted the sum. She took it into her hand and almost gulped, then quavered, "Would you like these gift wrapped?"

Roan shook his head, extending his hand for the box the woman held ready to slip into a bag for him. When the woman faltered, Roan reached over and extracted the box from her hand, then turned his back on her and walked out of the shop, leaving her to stare after him with a bewildered, thoughtful look.

Within minutes Roan was back in the motel room, uncustomarily uncertain as to whether he was glad or sorry that Gem still slept on. Characteristically, however, he gave a shrug of his wide shoulders, placed the box on the dresser, picked up the note he had left and slipped it into his pocket, failing to note that as he did so one of his business cards fluttered to the floor. He then penned a new note, slid it under the jeweler's box, then walked to the side of the bed to stare down at Gem for a long moment. He found himself stretching out a hand to gently touch the black sheen of her hair; then, as if impatient with himself, he drew back, turned on his heel, and left the room again to go about his business with a clear conscience and a determination to put Gem Reasoner out of his mind as thoroughly and as quickly as he had every other woman he had ever left sleeping in a bed he had helped tousle.

When Gem came blinking awake an hour or so later, she was at first disoriented at finding herself in a strange motel room. Then a slow, sweet smile of anticipation curved her slightly swollen lips as she moved quietly to turn over and face the other side of the bed. Disappointment chased the smile away when she saw the empty space beside her, and she reached a hesitant hand to touch the depression in the pillow beside her own. An ache of loneliness besieged her as the quiet in the room told her Roan had gone.

Perhaps he had just gone to breakfast or for some coffee? The thought brought her upright with a surge of energy, and she was out of bed, trying to find her purse to extract her comb and bring some semblance of order to her tousled hair before he returned. But as she moved to the dresser her eyes caught the small velvet box with a slip of white paper under it, and she paused, a sense of dread invading her to replace the energetic well-being she had been experiencing a mere second ago.

It took fortitude to reach out and take that note into her hand. Characteristically it was the note, not the jeweler's box, she reached for first. Her jaw tightened, and a pained look chased the sleep-softened gray from her eyes to turn it to the slate of a thunder-ridden sky. She read the note twice, and then its contents were embedded in her heart forever.

> I was overpaid for my protection. Allow me to bring things into balance again. I hope these are compatible with the charming pendant you wear and that they will bring to mind a most pleasurable night whenever you wear them.
>
> Roan

Head bowed, Gem surveyed her nude body with contempt, noting the very slight bruising on her breasts and thighs that was evidence of the strength of Roan's passion the night before. Then, with a sick feeling of inevitability, she reached for the velvet box and flipped open the lid to survey the contents with cold disgust. Nestled against the dark velvet were two exquisite earrings consisting of a large, clear emerald surrounded by a cluster of dainty, sparkling diamonds. The things were obviously expensive, but their cost to Gem was far higher than what Roan had paid for them.

She snapped the lid back down hastily and threw the box back onto the dresser as though it were contaminated. Then she crossed to the bathroom, where she turned on the taps and activated the shower. Gem scrubbed her body as though she were filthy, while her mind deliberated with cold calmness.

There was no way she could explain to herself how she had fallen prey to Roan Christianson's brand of seduction so quickly and so thoroughly. She must simply accept that she *had* done so and now must face the consequences of her own self-contempt. His opinion of her had been made clear by the note and the gift. To him she was little better than an expensive call girl. She thought with wry, dark humor that she supposed she should be grateful his opinion of her was that high. The way she felt at the moment, she thought she only deserved a few crumpled dollar bills, if anything at all.

And then her customary self-respect asserted itself, and by the time Gem climbed outside the shower to wrap herself in a large white towel, she had turned her anger outward instead of inward. The anger was not that of a woman scorned, but rather contempt for a man who had so little discernment that he couldn't tell the difference between a woman who gave herself from genuine passion and one who expected payment for her services. He was obviously experienced, and yet he hadn't been able to detect that Gem herself was not.

Whereas before, she had felt devastated that Roan hadn't had the common decency to wake her to say good-bye, she now considered it typical of his crude character and was grateful she had been spared from showing him the feelings that had enveloped her upon awaking. She felt certain she would have made a complete fool of herself.

Gem dressed with the haste of someone who wanted to get away from an unpleasant experience, as indeed she did. She wanted to put this town and Roan Christianson behind her, and she wished her softheartedness and her stubborn pride had never made it necessary to encounter either. But then she remembered

Billy, and she realized she was not sorry she had been instrumental in maintaining his faith in his father.

Even her night with Roan was good for something, she thought grimly as she put on her clothes. He had shown her what a skilled, attractive man bent on seduction could accomplish, and in the process he had taught her the possibilities of her own sexuality. The first would increase her inherent wariness of the male sex in general, while the second would provide a guide for finding a *decent* man to marry and establish a family with.

Gem approached the dresser to retrieve her purse, and as her eyes fell on the jeweler's box again, she bit her lip, wondering what she should do with Roan's unwelcome gift. She wanted to throw it in the trash, but her common sense told her that was a foolish gesture. Then her eyes found the white square of Roan's business card at her feet, and she bent to retrieve it. Her gray eyes widened as she saw the name of his company, recognized it, and took in the fact that Roan Christianson owned it.

She tapped the card on her palm for a moment, thinking hard, and then a slow smile lifted the corners of her mouth, and her eyes began to sparkle with pleasure as an idea formed in her head. She dropped the card and the jeweler's box in her purse, swung around toward the door, paused momentarily to stare at the tousled bed with a grim look of remembrance, and then she left the room to make her way back to her home . . . and to people who would recognize her worth and love her even had she not deserved it.

CHAPTER FIVE

The little green pickup sped along the country road, responding to Gem's desire to be done with these last few miles and to see her family for the first time in two years. Her attempt to expunge the memory of the preceding night from her consciousness had been only partially successful, but she was certain that once she had disposed of Roan's "gift," she would be able to wipe out every trace of him from her mind. Never had she been more glad than now that she was protected from any other unwelcome consequences of her night of madness. Traveling alone as she had been, she had taken steps to make sure that if there ever came a time when her independence resulted in being taken advantage of, she would not be caught unawares. She thought it ironic that that protection had been unnecessary until the very last night of her sojourn, and that if she hadn't had it, she might not have succumbed to Roan's spell so easily.

Her heart quickened as the long drive leading to her family's sprawling ranch came into sight, and she slowed to make the turn, remembering countless other times when she had done so. The family had a home in Dallas as well, but it was here that she had spent most of her childhood and formed her fondest memories.

The Spanish-style house came into view, and Gem's palms went moist with anticipation and excitement. She hoped they would both be there—her father and her mother. She wanted nothing to spoil this homecoming. But though she had called and alerted the housekeeper, Rosita, to the approximate time of her arrival, she had been unable to speak to one of the family, as they were both away at the time.

Suddenly she was a little girl again when she saw the tall, powerful form of her father emerge from the wide front doors just as she brought the pickup to a stop in front of the house. She was out of the driver's seat before the engine had stopped chugging, and flying around the front of the pickup to launch herself into her father's strong arms, just as she had every time she'd greeted him from her toddler days.

"Daddy!" Gem cried in a choked voice full of the tears misting her eyes. "Oh, Daddy!" Her tone said it all—her love for him, her joy at being with him again, the security she felt having his arms around her.

"There, sweetheart. There now . . ." Big Jim Reasoner's voice was choked as well as he hugged to him his only daughter, the treasure he had worried over for the past two years while refusing to show that worry to anyone. Instead, typically, he had expressed his pride in her independence along with a rueful lack of understanding of why she felt she had to express it in such a drastic manner. But then, Big Jim, while fully aware of his ability to intimidate the businessmen and ranchers he dealt with daily, was unaware that his powerful personality could smother those he loved as well.

After a few moments of mutual pleasure in holding each other again, Big Jim finally pushed his daughter away to arm's length to study her with shrewd, loving, perceptive gray eyes that were so like those that looked joyfully back at him.

"You went away from me a little girl," he murmured huskily. "I think you've come back a woman, and I'm not sure I like that."

Gem couldn't help the blush that feathered her silken cheeks becomingly, her father's words recalling to her the fact that if she now appeared to be a woman in his eyes, her experiences with Roan Christianson the night before had no doubt had a lot to do with her transformation.

"We all have to grow up sometime, Daddy," she said softly,

letting her own loving gaze take an inventory of the changes in her father while she'd been gone. She thought she detected a few more flecks of gray in his still-dark thickly waving hair, and a few more lines in his craggy, powerful face. "You look wonderful," she said sincerely. "Maybe a little more gray?" she teased him with tender mischief.

"If I am, you put it there," her father admitted with gruff emotion in his deep voice. "In my day a girl child didn't feel it necessary to run off from her family and travel the whole damned country by herself." As he half-scolded her he took her under the protection of his strong right arm and turned her toward the house.

"Come on, Daddy," Gem mocked him severely. "How many times have you told me the story about Grandma Reasoner and how she left her home in civilized St. Louis to travel down here to the wilds of Texas with Grandpa."

"Hmph!" Jim Reasoner refused to give an inch. "She was with her husband, though, wasn't she? Not all alone."

"It was still a big step," Gem asserted stoutly. "And I'm back all in one piece, aren't I?" She stilled the small twinge of conscience that troubled her as she remembered Roan Christianson. "I've got some big news for you too," she hastened on, letting her voice convey some of her inner pride. "But just for your scolding, I'm going to make you wait for it until Mom can hear it too."

"Ha! Ten to one it's something your mother won't want to hear," her father predicted with a conspiratorial twinkle in his eye that referred to his wife's gentle snobbishness.

"I know," Gem said with a peal of silvery laughter. "That's what's going to be so much fun about it."

"Well, you're gonna have to wait till dinner to tell me, then," Big Jim said with a laugh, a sly look in his eyes. "Your mom's off at one of those goldarned meetings of hers and won't be back till then. Think you can hold out till she's home?"

He looked disappointed when Gem asserted that she could,

indeed, hold off. "But I wish she was here," Gem complained disappointedly. "Didn't she know when I was coming?"

"Yeah, she knew," Big Jim said as he closed the door behind the two of them. "I think this is her way of telling you she doesn't approve of what you did."

Gem shrugged and rolled her eyes. "She told me that quite plainly before I left," she said with dry ruefulness. "I got the message then."

"Well, you know your mom always likes to make her point." Big Jim chuckled, watching his daughter fondly as she gazed around at her former home with eagerness.

"You haven't changed anything," Gem breathed with satisfaction. "I'm so glad."

"I wouldn't let her," Big Jim said in an implacable tone. "I knew you'd want to come home to what you left."

"Thanks, Daddy," Gem said softly, feeling a tinge guilty at knowing that her father had taken up the cudgels with her mother, who was known for her sudden flights of interior decorating.

"Yes, well, I couldn't stop her at the house in Dallas," he admitted sheepishly. "But I figured you wouldn't care so much about it there."

"You're right." Gem laughed. "I always considered this home."

She and her father made a quick tour so Gem could see in detail that nothing had changed, and then Gem went to her old room while her father made some telephone calls, a practice he couldn't delay for long wherever they were or whatever the time. Gem sat on the yellow coverlet on her white bed and gazed with fond remembrance at the girlish room where she had dreamed girlish dreams of becoming a famous songwriter . . . one dream which was on the verge of coming true if the public liked the songs she had sold. Other dreams—in particular one of finding her knight in shining armor—were as yet unfulfilled.

A slight tug of sadness made Gem's sweetly formed mouth turn downward for an instant as she remembered Roan Christianson. He had started out like that proverbial knight, rescuing her from danger the way he had, but he had soon turned into just another modern man on the make. Determinedly Gem shrugged away her thoughts and jumped up to visit the row of Raggedy Ann dolls which stood arrayed on a white wicker chest. She touched a finger to each one, reflecting that she was, indeed, a woman now. There was no place for dolls in her life. And if she knew anything at all about her parents, she knew they would resume their determined efforts to get her married off to someone suitable so she could produce real live babies.

She sighed as she felt her childhood leaving her for good, to be replaced by the adult concerns and responsibilities of any other woman. If she had her way, she would put off taking on those particular responsibilities having to do with love and marriage and children for a while. She wanted to savor her career for a time on her own. And when she did decide to settle down, it would be with a man of *her* choice, not her father's and certainly not her mother's.

An hour later she came to the dining room just as her mother entered it, and the two of them stood for a long moment gazing at each other, fondness and mutual irritation evident on their identical faces, though their features were framed by different hairstyles of a different color.

Finally Audra Reasoner held out her arms to her daughter. "I'm glad you're home," she said simply in a husky voice that so resembled Gem's.

Gem ran to her mother and hugged her enthusiastically, then stepped back to run her eyes over the designer gown her parent wore with such style. "You look as good as ever," Gem said with a laugh, and then, "Don't say it! I meant to change from my jeans, but the time got away from me."

One of her mother's patrician eyebrows rose sceptically, but she seemed disinclined to comment on Gem's informal attire. She did not, however, refrain from commenting on her hairstyle. "You need a visit to the hairdresser in the worst way. How long has it been since you had that mane cut?"

Gem tossed back the length of her black, softly waving hair, and her expression teased her mother. "I couldn't afford many visits to a hairdresser on my budget," she said solemnly, noting with inner glee the pained expression in her mother's blue eyes, "and besides, no one can do me justice like Charles can. I'll make an appointment with him the next time we go to Dallas, I promise."

"I should hope so," her mother replied sternly. "And I expect you need to visit some shops for clothes as well?" Now her expression as she ran her cool blue eyes over Gem's dusty jeans and plaid shirt was definitely disdainful.

"Could be," Gem replied with a noncommittal shrug. "You can vet my clothes for me when I get unpacked." Then she determinedly turned the conversation away from her wardrobe and her hairstyle. "Is dinner almost ready?" she asked, sniffing and reveling in the smell of hot, spicy Mexican food that pervaded the air. "Is Rosita cooking tonight?" she asked eagerly.

"I expect so," her mother answered with a wry moue on her vermilion lips. "She spoils you as badly as your father does, and she knows all your favorites."

"Oh, God!" Gem placed her hands over her mouth in consternation. "I haven't even seen her yet. She wasn't in the kitchen when I looked earlier. I'd better pop in, or her feelings will be hurt."

"Undoubtedly." Her mother gave her a chastizing look. "Run along, then, while I locate your father."

Gem hastened toward the source of the appetizing smells that had caught her attention, and when she passed into the beautifully appurtenanced Spanish-style kitchen, her eyes flew immediately to the stout figure of a middle-aged woman stirring something on the stove.

Gem tiptoed up behind the woman, and when she was directly behind her, she said in a plaintive, little girl voice, "I'm hungry, Rosita. Could I have a cookie, please?"

The woman swung around, her weathered face already creased in a thousand places with the warmth of her smile. She held up a stern finger and tried to force a frown onto her beaming face. "No cookie, *niña,*" she said in a scolding tone. "It will spoil your dinner."

And then the two of them were laughing and hugging, and Gem felt truly at home enfolded in those plump, motherly arms which had held her so often in the past. Rosita finally did exactly as Gem's mother and father had, holding her off for a thorough inspection.

"You're skin and bones," she said, shaking her head in consternation. "Did you not have money enough to eat, little one?"

Gem laughed, breaking away to do a pirouette in front of her second mother. "Don't you know the slender look is stylish, Rosita? You want me to catch a man, don't you?"

"Hmph!" Rosita was unconvinced. "No Spanish man would want such a skeleton, I can tell you that!" And then she shooed Gem away toward the dining room. "But I will fix it, don't worry. We will put some flesh on those bones so a man will have something to warm him on a cold night."

Gem's laugh broke through her mock grimace. "If it will make you happy, Rosita, I'll see if I can eat a *little* of that terribly fattening dinner you're fixing."

"Humph!" Rosita fixed her with a knowing dark eye. "If I remember right, you will do more than eat a little. You will clean up your plate and ask for seconds, and then demand some dessert!"

Gem hung her head in mock shame. "Oh, Rosita," she said sorrowfully. "I have no secrets from you, do I?"

Hands on hips, Rosita forsook her teasing for a wisely speculative look. "I would not be too sure of *that,*" she said archly. "You are no longer a little girl, I think."

Gem couldn't help the revealing flush that stained her cheeks, but she managed a flippant answer. "Of course not, Rosita! I'm all grown up now, and I'll have some news for all of you to prove it after dinner."

Her diversion proved effective, as she had known it would. Rosita could never resist anything that smacked of secrecy, and as Gem had made a point of imparting a secretive tone to her message, Rosita fell for it. She clapped her hands like an overgrown child. "Oh, good! I knew things would liven up around here when you got back."

Backing toward the door, Gem gave a mock bow. "I'm always happy to serve, Senora," she said formally with a dramatic sweep of her hand.

"Get along with you, then," Rosita retorted, turning back to her cooking. "I want to get this dinner served so I can hear what you've been up to."

Gem departed from the room, wondering with a sense of irritated chagrin how those who knew and loved her so well could pick up so immediately on the change in her. Did a single night of sin mark one with a scarlet letter?

An hour or so later Gem lay back on the sofa cushions in the family room feeling so full, it was a definite effort to expend the energy to breathe, much less move. The dinner had been one of Rosita's best efforts, and the reunion at table had been full of laughter and affection as Gem recounted some of her adventures with enough exaggeration to make her mother sigh repeatedly and her father's laugh boom out continuously. And now it was time for the big news, and Gem wished she hadn't expended most of her energy on the small news and Rosita's good cooking.

"All right," her father said, bringing matters to a head. "What is this news you're holding back from us? Are you engaged to a millionaire or something?"

Gem grimaced, then laughed. "Nothing so spectacular, Daddy. But before I tell you, call Rosita. I promised she could hear too."

Her father did as she asked with ill-disguised impatience, and when all three of them sat facing her with varying degrees of anticipation evident on their expressive faces, Gem made the effort to sit up and give them what they wanted.

"I sold my songs," she informed them with quiet satisfaction. "To a publisher in Nashville. For a lot of money." Then she sat back to await their reactions.

They weren't slow in coming. Her father was immediately proud of her, but with reservations. "Good girl," he said heartily, and then, more cautiously, "What do you call a 'lot of money'?"

Gem laughed and told him, enjoying immensely the look of surprised respect she saw on his face. Of course, the amount was a drop in the bucket compared to the resources he controlled, but it was so much more than he had expected, she knew he was pleased for her.

Rosita merely looked proudly complacent, as though she had known all along that her *niña* would attain her goal. It was her mother's reaction that astonished Gem.

"Good," she said with a great deal of satisfaction in her tone. "I'm glad you've got that out of your system now."

Gem's pleasure in her mother's acceptance was tinged with caution. "What do you mean, 'out of my system'?" she asked suspiciously.

Her mother sat back and contemplated her long vermillion fingernails with interest. "I mean, now that you've proven you can be a success at something, you can get on with your life, can't you?"

"What do you mean by getting on with my life?" Gem asked dryly. "And selling my songs doesn't mean I'm a success. It just means I have a chance to become a success. The listening public will make the final decision, and if they don't like what I've written, no song publisher is likely to buy any more of my songs."

Her mother fixed her with a cool look from under her patrician brows. "By getting on with your life I mean getting married and having children." She ignored Gem's heavy sigh and said carefully, "Did you know Bobby Joe Owens is still asking about you?"

A fond smile curved Gem's mouth as she remembered Bobby Joe. She had dated him throughout high school, and indeed, it was with him that Gem had first engaged in experimenting with sex, though the attempt had proven to be a disaster. She had managed to lose her virginity, but with very little ecstasy as a byproduct. It had taken Roan Christianson to break through the barriers Gem had set against any further disasters of that kind.

"How is Bobby Joe?" she asked with the comfortable interest she would shown in any other of her old friends. Mentally she shook her head in wry resignation as she saw her mother regard her inquiry as a sign of more interest than she felt.

"He's doing quite well for himself," Audra Reasoner said complacently. "I understand he's a first-rate lawyer now."

"I'll have to call him when we go to Dallas," Gem replied matter-of-factly. "Maybe we can get the old gang together for an evening out."

That seemed to satisfy her mother for the time being, and after another hour or so of discussing Gem's career and of catching up on family news, everyone opted for an early night, as Audra Reasoner had arbitrarily decided that since her husband planned a trip to Dallas the next day anyway, she and Gem would accompany him.

"Take enough clothes for a few days, Gem," she had instructed her daughter in her imperious fashion. "You'll have to accompany your father to the annual Oil and Gas Dinner, because I'm off to Paris for the fashion shows in a few days."

Since it was her first day back home, Gem elected to eschew any arguement over her mother's dictatorial arrangements for the time being. But as she got ready for bed that night she knew the time was fast approaching when she would have to take a stand and assert her independence again, and she sighed when she contemplated her parents' reaction to the news that she planned to find herself an apartment of her own in the very near future.

CHAPTER SIX

As Roan Christianson picked up his very beautiful, very fashionable date for the Oil and Gas Dinner, he noted the long, dangling diamond earrings hanging from her ears, and the sight reminded him of the curious letter he had gotten in the mail that day from a local charity thanking him for his most generous gift of a pair of diamond and emerald earrings and informing him of the amount he should deduct from his taxes as a result of that gift.

He had known immediately, of course, the source of the gift, but what puzzled him was why it had been made and how the real donor had known who he was and his address, so that the gift could be made in his name. He had to admit, if only to himself and grudgingly, that the action piqued his vanity somewhat. He had thought the young woman he had spent that most pleasurable night with recently would have needed the money herself, or else why would she have been singing in such a place to earn a salary? He had also to admit that it had given him pleasure to think of her wearing his gift and remembering that night each time she did. Almost he wished he had found out more about her. She had been preying on his mind, which was a totally unusual reaction to a woman for him, and an affair with her might have, when it was over, erased that annoying tendency he had to think of her at the oddest and most inopportune times. Like now, for instance, when his date was visibly pouting at his lack of attentiveness.

Sometime later, when the two of them had arrived at the dinner and Roan had effectively erased his date's pout, he was half-listening to her chatter as he assessed the other guests and made up his mind whom he would approach to talk a little business with. Suddenly his powerful frame tensed, and his gold-flecked eyes widened as he caught sight of a couple just entering the doorway to the vast room where the dinner was being held.

Big Jim Reasoner was a man to command attention at any time from a man of Roan's sort, but it was not Big Jim Roan was staring at. It was the finely boned, black-haired, beautiful creature who clung to Big Jim's arm. Roan's eyes narrowed as he took in the lovely designer creation Gem wore and calculated its price. His eyes then focused on the elaborate hairstyle Gem had adopted for the evening and the diamond bracelet flashing on her arm when she raised her hand to smooth that hairstyle.

One dark eyebrow rose in speculation as Roan tried to make sense of the fact that this woman, who had been on his mind so often after a night of passion he found it impossible to forget, was here with one of the wealthiest, best known oil-and-cattle men in Texas. He wanted to believe Gem was Big Jim's mistress, but he knew the man's reputation well, and there had never been a hint that Reasoner indulged in that sort of thing. And even if he had, it was doubtful he would bring a mistress to this sort of function.

A hard smile tugged at one corner of Roan's beautifully chiseled mouth as he made up his mind to accomplish two objectives at once. He would meet the nymph who still plagued his thoughts so persistently, and he would solve the mystery of why she was here with Jim Reasoner. With that objective in mind Roan began to subtly move his date in the direction the couple who interested him so had taken.

Gem was already rather glassy-eyed from the introductions and idle chatter she had had to endure since she and her father had arrived at this, to her, exceptionally boring function. She felt both resentment at her absent mother for sticking her with this duty and embarrassment at her father's irrepressible tendency to brag about her to all of his old cronies. And most of them *were* old. She would not even be able to talk to people of her own age to enliven what promised to be a very long evening indeed.

She was taking a sip from her glass of wine to conceal an irrepressible sigh of resignation when out of the corner of her eye she glimpsed the well-remembered figure of Roan Christianson making his way inexorably toward her with a really stunning blonde in tow. Choking on her wine, Gem frantically turned her back on the man bearing down on her, trying to regain the composure that had fled immediately upon spotting Roan and realizing he meant to confront her here . . . in front of her father, no less!

Oh, God! She sought frantically for some means of escape. Could she disappear on the excuse of finding a powder room? But would that only delay the inevitable? Would Roan acknowledge that he knew her, or would he have the decency to pretend he was meeting her for the first time?

Time ran out as she heard her father greeting the man she least wanted to see at this particular moment . . . or at any moment, for that matter!

"Roan!" Jim Reasoner's deep bass rang out clearly. "Where have you been keeping yourself these days? I've tried to call you a couple of times on that Roberts lease, but you weren't in."

"You should have left word," came the well-remembered deep tones Gem had dreaded to hear. "I would have returned your call, though there's nothing to report as yet. I haven't been able to get Roberts to sign on the dotted line so far."

"Ah, well, he will," Gem's father asserted confidently. "He's just holding out for all he can get." And then, as she had dreaded, she felt her father's hand on her arm turning her toward Roan and Roan's date. "Have you met my daughter, Roan?" Big Jim asked proudly. "She's just home from wandering the country for a couple of years."

Bracing herself, Gem slowly raised wary gray eyes to Roan's mocking brown ones. She held her breath as she waited for Roan to indicate whether he had, or had not, met her before, and then almost let it out in a rush of relief at his reply.

"Why, no," he drawled charmingly, "I don't believe I have." Only Gem saw or understood the slight drooping of his left eyelid in a partial wink.

"Gem, this is Roan Christianson," Jim Reasoner announced happily. "And you're Bob Grimm's daughter, aren't you?" he asked, turning to the blonde on Roan's arm.

"This is Fala Grimm," Roan said smoothly as he dipped his head down toward his date. The blonde nodded haughtily at Gem and more politely at Jim Reasoner.

"My daughter's a songwriter," Jim Reasoner said, starting on what had become a well-rehearsed spiel for him that evening, "and she's just signed—"

"Daddy!" Gem interrupted him rather more sharply than she had meant to, then softened it by giving her father a warm smile. "I believe Mr. Owens is trying to get your attention." The supposed Mr. Owens, a name Gem had seized on in a burst of desperate inspiration, was not Bobby Joe's father at all; but simply a bald-headed, portly gentleman who had been looking vaguely in their direction.

"Who?" Jim Reasoner's puzzlement was evident in his tone as he craned his head in the direction Gem indicated.

"Over there," Gem said firmly, trying unobtrusively to push her father in the direction she wanted him to go.

Jim Reasoner frowned down at his daughter for a second, then shrugged as he gave Roan and his date an apologetic smile. "See you at dinner, Roan?" he managed to get in before Gem could drag him completely away.

"Oh, most assuredly," Roan said with a note of steel in his voice as his eyes glinted a warning at Gem. "And for the dancing later as well," he added in a tone that was a promise.

Gem just stopped herself from grimacing at her tormentor, and as she and her father left the man who had her pulses pounding from three feet away, she did allow herself a long breath of relief.

"Who's this Owens you're talking about?" her father asked

rather grumpily, still searching the faces of the crowd around him.

"Oh?" Gem managed to look surprised. "Isn't that Mr. Owens?" she asked guilelessly as she pointed out the stranger who had served her purposes unknowingly.

"Hell, no!" Jim Reasoner said with emphatic impatience. "That's old Wildcat Baker, and I'm damned if I want to get caught up in any of his endless tales of the old days." He fixed Gem with a stern scowl, and Gem patted his arm placatingly.

"Sorry, Daddy," she said with innocent sweetness. "My mistake."

Jim opened his mouth to remonstrate with her further, but fortunately another acquaintance claimed his attention at that moment, and Gem was subjected to yet another embarrassing spiel from her father about her new fame. When they finally managed to break free, Gem instructed her proud papa in no uncertain terms that she had had more than enough of his subjecting her to such recitations. Her father looked offended for a moment, but he took note of her objections and refrained from any further demonstrations of fatherly pride.

By the time it was expected of everyone to file in for dinner, Gem was desperate for some way to escape another meeting with Roan Christianson, but short of pleading some sort of desperate illness she could come up with nothing that would save her from enduring not only the baiting of those relentless eyes of his but her undiminished attraction to his physical appeal. She had felt despair at realizing her reaction to him was every bit as potent as it had been on the night he had seduced her, but she was determined not to give in to his appeal again. He had shown his true colors the proverbial "morning after," and she knew instinctively that he represented nothing but heartache and danger for her if she let herself succumb to him in any way at all.

She almost groaned when her father steered her to a table for four at which Roan and his date were already seated, and she unconsciously pulled back on Jim Reasoner's strong arm. But upon seeing the puzzled, impatient look her father gave her, she knew she couldn't come up with any excuse not to sit with Roan that would satisfy her parent, and with a sense of dread fatalism she allowed herself to be seated a bare few inches from the man she had thought never to see again.

The look Roan turned on her reminded her of some dangerous jungle beast preparing to play with his trapped dinner before devouring it whole. The look his date turned on her was that of a waspish insect preparing to plunge its deadly stinger straight into her heart. Gem smiled faintly at the two of them, sighed inwardly, and prepared to endure.

Fortunately Jim Reasoner saw no reason to regard the occasion as strictly social and launched immediately into a business discussion with Roan that Gem hoped had diverted his attention from her. She was proven wrong when she felt his warm hand suddenly descend onto her knee and begin a stroking caress that had her sitting bolt upright one moment and longing to slide under the table the next.

"Something wrong?" Gem heard Roan's solicitous drawl through a haze of sensuality during a break in the conversation as the waiter served them appetizers. "You look a little pale."

Gem forced herself to look at Roan's innocently bland expression without the hostility she would have liked to show him. "No . . ." she faltered, dismayed to hear her voice break. "I . . . er . . . ah . . . have a slight headache, that's all," she finished as she saw her father's concerned gaze focus on her.

"A headache?" Jim Reasoner boomed out in a tone that made Gem wince. "You never have headaches! Is this something you picked up in your travels?"

Before she could answer, Roan interrupted smoothly. "Ah, yes," he said, beaming at her with fake interest, "I believe Jim was starting to tell us about your career when you were . . . ah . . . called away earlier." His seemingly innocent hesitation told Gem her earlier eagerness to get away from him had not gone unnoted.

"It's nothing," she said with almost grim shortness. "I'm sure you and Daddy have other things to discuss that are much more interesting."

Both men denied this simultaneously, and Gem closed her eyes briefly in resignation as her father launched into his proud dissertation on his daughter's talent while Roan listened very politely.

"I can understand why you're so proud of her, Jim," he said suavely when Gem's father had temporarily run down. "I understand it takes a lot of talent to sell anything in that market these days."

Gem almost writhed in embarrassment when she remembered the only time Roan Christianson had had occasion to judge that talent. She remembered vividly that he had been singularly unimpressed during her performance at that loathsome club the night she'd met him, and she couldn't blame him. The atmosphere had been so wrong from the beginning that she had not been at her best, to say the least.

"Do you sing as well as write music, Gem?" Roan's question was delivered as smoothly as a well-honed knife between her ribs.

Gem stared back at the mocking humor in those distinctive brown eyes fringed with long, thick lashes that somehow managed to be anything but feminine, her own gray stare shimmering with challenge. "Yes, I do," she said in a clipped tone, refusing to elaborate further, daring him to do so.

"You mean you sing in nightclubs?" The slightly sneering tone in the blonde's question put Gem's back up, but as she swung her gaze to the questioner to answer, her look was calmly regal.

"I have, yes," she said levelly. "That's how I made my living for the last two years. But it was more to make expenses and try out some of my songs than from inclination. I don't plan to make singing a career."

"Why would you want a career at all?" the blonde persisted, her blue gaze dismissing of Gem's ambition and barely civil.

Gem smiled sweetly at her, by now, recognized adversary. "I

don't happen to like living off of anyone, not even my father," she said gently. "It smacks too much of being . . . kept."

"Gem!" Her father protested his daughter's gently worded rebuke halfheartedly, though his gray eyes shone with suppressed laughter, as he considered the rebuke well deserved. "What a thing to say!"

Gem knew her father's remonstrance was more a matter of form than conviction, and so she adopted a suitable expression of repentance. "Sorry, Daddy," she murmured placatingly, then risked a glance at Roan to see his reaction to his date's baiting of her and her subsequent put-down of his date. She was not reassured when she saw his eyes dancing with wicked enjoyment. Did he have no loyalty to his date, she wondered? But, of course, he wouldn't, she thought cynically a second later. Roan was a user of women, not a man who appreciated them for their special worth.

Then, as she caught sight of the hostile coldness in Fala Grimm's glittering blue eyes, she decided that not all females were worthy of the respect Roan refused to give any of them.

The conversation turned desultory after that while they finished their meal, though Gem felt anything but calm, since Roan took every occasion to brush his thigh against hers, to hold her gaze with his own when she made the mistake of looking his way, and to make her aware, nonverbally, that he wasn't finished with her yet. Why he shouldn't be, she didn't know. He had certainly made it clear he was finished with her the morning after she'd spent the night in his arms, hadn't he? Was his discovery of her parentage making him reassess her? If he thought she was going to be fool enough to let him resume his humiliating domination of her senses, he had another think coming, she resolved determinedly.

That resolution proved easier to make than to keep as the evening wore on, however. The first time Roan asked her to dance, she accepted with outward calmness, planning to use the opportunity to make him aware that there could be nothing between them now. But as his arm closed around her waist and drew her stiff form to his long, muscled length, she felt every nerve come alive to his touch, and it was all she could do to keep from closing her eyes to revel in the sensation and leaning into him with submission.

Roan wasted no time in striking another sort of nerve. "I received acknowledgment of your gift in my name today," he murmured against her ear, his breath fanning a warmth in her she was struggling valiantly to control. "Were you soothing your conscience?" he asked, gentle amusement lurking in his low-voiced, sensuous tone.

Gem stiffened in his grasp, then relaxed consciously. "Why in the world should my conscience bother me?" she responded with a slightly bored air. "Does your conscience bother *you* after a one-night stand?" Her wryly sarcastic barb failed to find its mark. Roan merely lifted his head to look into her glacial eyes, his own softly speculative.

"My conscience almost never bothers me," he drawled mockingly. "But, then, I've had a lot more experience than you have."

Gem froze, missing a step in the dance, uncertain whether Roan meant that she had performed inadequately in bed due to her lack of experience, or whether he was genuinely perceptive enough to guess that her inexperience had given rise to a sense of guilt at having behaved so uncharacteristically with him.

Roan's smile as she recovered her balance infuriated her. "Don't be too sure of that," she said coldly. "How do you know I didn't mark you out for an evening's entertainment the moment I saw you that night in the club?"

"Honey," Roan said with just a hint of chastisement, "don't try to fool an old pro. You were fantastic, but nothing like you could be if we had time together to increase your . . . experience."

Gem turned stormy eyes to his, her mouth compressed into a tight line. "That isn't going to happen," she said with grim determination, electing to stop beating about the bush and get to the point as straightforwardly as he had.

"No?" Roan said softly, his warm brown gaze traveling her face possessively. "Why not? Are you afraid of growing up?"

"I *am* grown up," Gem asserted hostily. "Enough to know better than to get involved with a man like you. You're a user, Roan Christianson. I wouldn't be surprised if you regarded women the way a rancher regards his cows. Something worthwhile only in relation to what he can get out of them, not as creatures with souls and minds and feelings."

Roan pursed his mouth speculatively, his eyes assessing as he studied Gem's stiff countenance. "No, you aren't grown up yet, honey," he said very softly. "Not when you haven't yet accepted that the things that can happen between a man and a woman don't have to be based on childish emotion."

His words confirmed her opinion of him, and Gem stared back at him, unaware of the bleak acceptance in her gaze. "Why this sudden interest, Roan?" she asked with quiet mockery. "You left me that morning without even bothering to say good-bye, expecting never to see me again. Does the fact that I'm Jim Reasoner's daughter have anything to do with your willingness to renew your acquaintance with me?"

For the first time since Roan had faced down Rawlins, Gem saw a return of that hard ruthlessness to his rugged face and of the cold anger to his eyes. His grip on her hand and waist tightened painfully, but Gem kept herself from wincing and returned Roan's look stoically, though she felt a dart of real fear at his expression.

"I don't need Jim Reasoner," Roan bit out with convincing harshness. "I've made it on my own all my life through hard work and brains and determination. I don't want anything I don't earn myself."

Gem believed him, even respected him, though she felt even more bleak at the picture he drew of himself as a man who didn't need love or people or any of the more human emotions most people couldn't live without. It was at that moment that she hardened her heart against his appeal and her body against its instinctive submission to Roan's.

"Well, you can't earn me, Roan," she answered with softly firm determination. "I'm not interested in what you have to offer. Will you take me back to the table now? I don't think we have anything more to discuss."

Instantly Roan's expression reverted back to gentle mockery. "No," he said, his soft tone failing to cloak the determination he felt. "I want you. I intend to have you. You want me; if you're honest, you'll admit it. I've decided to take your education in hand. In fact, I'm looking forward to it."

Gem felt a sense of despair as she realized he meant what he said. He *wanted* her, the way some men might want money or success or a piece of land. She only hoped she could stand up against the ruthless determination she instinctively recognized in his character to get what he wanted at any cost.

"I don't play games, Roan," she said quietly, holding his gaze, her eyes stony with her own determination. "I don't want an affair with you." She shrugged at the disbelief in his eyes. "I didn't say you can't make me want you physically. You know you can. I know it too. But we have different philosophies, I'm afraid. I'm not interested in casual relationships. I won't give in."

Inwardly she quailed at his answer to the challenge she had offered him. "We'll see, honey," he murmured with easy humor. "I've shown you before that what you intend is not what you really want. I'll do it again."

"No . . ." Gem started to continue her protest, then dropped it, her shoulders relaxing slightly, indicating her weary acceptance that words would mean nothing to Roan. It was her actions that would convince him . . . if anything could. She shrugged, holding his gaze and tilting her chin up, the battle lines clearly drawn.

CHAPTER SEVEN

The next evening Gem sat in grim silence beside her father in the silver Mercedes, speeding on her way to a destination she would have sworn just twenty-four hours earlier nothing could make her seek. She had questioned her father about Roan Christianson the night before on their way home, feeling ambiguous about the answers she had gotten.

Jim Reasoner obviously respected and liked Roan, which should have been an accolade, as Gem's father was a shrewd and hard-nosed judge of other men. But, then, the qualities he valued were not the same as those Gem considered important.

Her father had teased her about her interest, seeming pleased that she had found Roan sufficiently impressive to spark that interest. "He's a good catch," Jim Reasoner had slyly suggested, his gray eyes twinkling at his daughter. "He's rich, successful, handsome, and enough man to keep you in line."

Gem had been very careful to appear bored with her father's matchmaking, wondering wryly what her father would have thought if he had known Roan was far more interested in taking his daughter to bed than in marrying her. "I'm not in the market, Dad," she had answered calmly. "I'll gladly let some other woman have the benefit of all that sterling manhood." But even as she had said the words she had had to grit her teeth at the unwelcome surge of jealousy that had accompanied the idea of another woman marrying Roan . . . not that that was likely to happen, as she was certain marriage was not in Roan's plans.

It was too late to divert her father, however. Jim Reasoner had suddenly seemed taken with the idea of his beautiful daughter becoming involved with a man of Roan Christianson's quality, and when he had informed Gem that Roan had invited the two of them to a party the next night, Gem's attempted rebellion was given short shrift.

"He's an important business contact, Gem," Jim Reasoner had said with impressive sternness. Your mother's not here to go with me, and I think it's the least you can do to help me out this once. I don't ask all that much of you, do I?"

Gem had squirmed, torn between a sense of self-preservation and her duty to her always loving, always generous parent. "Dad, you can go alone, can't you? I have something else . . ."

But her father had been adamant. "It's a couples party, Gem. I can't go alone. Whatever you had planned can wait, can't it?"

From long experience Gem had recognized the signs that indicated her father was not to be swayed by any excuses she might be able to invent. He had that stubborn set to his jaw, and he was using the tone of voice that could make grown men quail; Gem was not proof against it, no matter how dangerous she was certain giving in to her father would prove to be to her. At least, she assured herself, she could probably avoid any close contact with Roan in a crowd at a party where he would have to perform a host's duties.

Now, as they sped through the night on their way to the last place Gem was certain she should be heading, she spent her time consolidating her defenses against the one man who had the necessary weapons to breach them. She concentrated on composing the lines to a song which spelled out her own inner conflict, a practice that had helped her cope with difficult situations in the past.

Just as they drove up a circular driveway to a home of impressive dimensions, the title of that song came to Gem, causing her lovely mouth to twist in a wry grimace of irony. *How can it feel so good to be so wrong?* echoed in her brain as she felt her nerves gathering taut in mingled excitement and dread.

A young man collected the car as Gem and her father went up the three steps to the front door, Jim Reasoner looking impressively handsome in a dark suit, white shirt, and red patterned tie, and Gem looking ethereally fragile in a flowing chiffon dress of mingled gray and white with dainty pearl earrings at her ears, her raven hair pulled back on one side with an ebony comb.

"You look beautiful, honey," Jim leaned down to whisper proudly to his daughter just as the door was opened to them by a tuxedoed butler.

"Thanks, Dad," Gem replied faintly, taking a deep breath and wondering if the modest cut of her dress had been a mistake after all. She had chosen it because she thought it hid most of her skin, not realizing that its flowing lines wrapped her body in tantalizing mystery certain to make a man want to unwrap it to find the source.

Roan appeared immediately as they came to the doorway of the huge room where the party was already in progress. "Good evening, Jim," he said with an easy friendliness before turning his liquid brown eyes on Gem in an assessment that left her feeling stripped to her soul.

She knew her cheeks pinkened in reaction to that look, but she kept her gray eyes tranquilly cool as Roan's gaze returned to her face. A muscle moved in his jaw while his eyes showed his satisfaction at her appearance.

"Hello, Gem," he said simply. "I'm glad you came."

I'll bet, Gem thought grimly as she let her soft lips form a polite smile. "Thank you, Roan," she said with grave civility. "You have a lovely home."

Gem's eyes denied the compliment, however, as did her tone. She found Roan's home pretentious and cold, entirely too formal to be a home, which was, perhaps, not surprising when he had no wife to make it one.

"Do you think so?" A new voice intruded into the conversation, and Gem swung around to find a younger, darker, gentler version of Roan standing at her side, looking at her with genuine puzzlement. "This place has always seemed like a mausoleum to me."

Gem's lips twitched in amusement as she saw that Roan had noted her own lack of sincerity in praising his home and that he was not pleased by her assessment. Neither was he pleased by the words spoken by the younger man who had joined them, as was evidenced by his wryly sardonic introduction.

"This is my little brother, Derek," Roan said as he inclined his head to the younger man. "He's an architect, and as you can see, his tastes are not traditional."

Gem shot the young man a look that plainly said, *Good for you,* but her reply to the introduction was blandly noncommittal. "How do you do, Derek?" she said with grave formality. "It's nice to meet you."

"I'm glad you said that," Derek said with a wide grin. "I have the feeling you're going to be the nicest thing to happen here tonight. Can I get you a drink?"

"No, you can't," Roan interjected with dry impatience. "I'll get Gem's drink. And you, Jim? What will you have?"

Jim Reasoner was grinning like a Cheshire cat at the rivalry between the brothers, his gleaming gray eyes evidencing unqualified enjoyment at the prospect of the two of them doing battle over his daughter. "Whiskey and water," he said jovially, placing a huge paw on Gem's shoulder to guide her after Roan as their host turned toward the bar set up at one end of the room. 'And Gem will have a vodka collins, right, Gem?"

"That will be fine," Gem acknowledged, her eyes sweeping Roan's distinctive, masculine profile of their own accord, finding pleasure in its strength even as her brain told her she would do well to keep her eyes off him and his undoubted appeal.

"I haven't seen you before." Derek Christianson claimed her attention again as he looked down at her admiringly. "How have I missed you?"

"I've been away for a couple of years," Gem replied easily, glad to have her attention diverted from Roan to this likable, safer version of maleness.

"I'm glad you're back." Derek grinned at her irrepressibly, ignoring the annoyed look his brother shot at him. "Will you dance with me later?"

"Certainly." Gem nodded her darkly shining head, her eyes teasing Derek in mild flirtation. "Look me up when you're ready."

"Oh, I'm ready now," Derek smiled back. "But Roan will kill me if he doesn't get the first dance. He's damned greedy." His chocolate-brown eyes openly mocked his brother as Roan looked at him with hard purpose. "Right, big brother?"

"Exactly right, little brother," Roan drawled easily. "And Sherri Brandon will kill you if you don't stop looking at Gem like a starving hound dog and get back over there to pay her some attention." His auburn head barely indicated a small red-headed, green-eyed imp glaring at them from across the room.

Derek merely laughed, then shrugged, gave Gem a deliberate wink, and slowly ambled over toward the redhead as though he had all the time in the world.

"I see Bob Miller's here," Jim Reasoner said with alacrity the moment he had his drink in hand. "Do you mind if I mosey over there and bend his ear a little, Roan? He's got a bull I'm wanting to use for stud service."

"By all means," Roan replied, his eyes on Gem as he spoke. "Consider my home as yours."

Gem took his meaning, but her reaction was perhaps different than Roan had planned. In the first place she didn't consider Roan's house a home, and in the second she was all too aware that he had not meant for her to consider his house a home in the sense a wife would. She wondered how many mistresses he had entertained in this huge mansion, and her eyes were frosty as she stared back at him.

"See you later, Gem," her father said as he strode rapidly away, leaving her to face Roan alone.

"Your father is most accommodating," Roan drawled as he reduced the space between him and Gem until his arm was brushing hers. "I might almost begin to think that he did that deliberately . . . leaving us alone, that is."

Gem faced him unflinchingly. "He did," she admitted casually. "My father has a heavy hand at matchmaking."

"Does that mean he thinks I'm a suitable catch?" Roan murmured, his hand snaking out to clasp Gem's, one thumb beginning to rub her palm with tantalizing suggestiveness.

"Oh, yes," Gem admitted again in a bored tone, letting her eyes roam the crowd and hoping Roan wouldn't move his grip to find that her pulse was racing madly. "He's unaware that your intentions don't include marriage. I think he might kill you if he knew what they really are."

Her threat failed to move Roan except to soft laughter. "I'm sure he'd like to," he chuckled. "And I'm equally sure you won't tell him."

"Are you?" Gem raised her eyebrows sceptically. "Why is that?"

"Because you want what's going to happen as badly as I do," Roan replied, a small quirk tugging at his sensuous mouth. "You just haven't admitted it to yourself yet."

Gem took a ragged breath as Roan's fingers wrapped around her wrist and found her racing pulse. It would be useless to deny his effect upon her, and she decided she wouldn't even try. She looked him directly in the eyes as she spoke, her own as calm as she could make them.

"You're wrong, Roan," she said levelly. "You feel my pulse. I admit freely what it's telling you. I want you more than I ever thought it possible to desire a man." She smiled wryly at Roan's look of deep satisfaction, tinged slightly with surprise at her honesty and beginning to shimmer with the desire she, in her turn, aroused in him.

"What you don't seem to understand is that I have no intention of giving in to that desire," Gem said with gentle firmness. "You're no good for me. I'm a woman who needs love, commitment . . . fidelity. You can't give me any of those things. You're not even prepared to try." She tugged at her wrist, releasing it from Roan's hold and stepping away from him. "Find some other woman to play your games with, Roan. I'm sure there are hundreds of them just waiting for the chance to play it your way."

And with that she turned her back on him, making her way across the room to a couple she had known since her childhood and who would provide a welcome refuge from the magnetism Roan exuded even in his anger. For he was angry, she knew, though he hid it well. What worried her more than his ire, however, was that steely look of indominitable purpose that had appeared in his eyes at the end of her little speech . . . a look that told her plainly she had not succeeded in making him abandon his pursuit of her body, but rather strengthened his determination to have it again, submissive to his demands.

She managed to avoid him after that, determinedly placing bodies between them whenever it looked as though he might head in her direction. Toward the middle of the evening, when she was about at the end of her rope with making small talk and keeping a wary eye out for the man who stalked her relentlessly with his eyes if not his body, Derek Christianson found her where she had retreated to a small alcove on an outside patio.

"There you are," he said with cheerful pleasure. "I was afraid you'd left before I got a chance to talk to you."

"No," Gem said with a dry smile. "I'm just tired of the small talk and needed some air." She moved over to make room for him on the small wrought iron bench. "Where's your friend?" she asked teasingly.

"Who's that?" Derek asked easily as he stretched out his long legs.

"The redhead . . . Sherri, wasn't it?"

Derek chuckled. "She's pouting in the ladies' room. She thinks I'm neglecting her."

"Are you?" Gem asked curiously, intrigued by Derek's easy manner. He seemed all of a piece, content with himself and the world around him, and in no way resembling his more dynamic brother.

"Yep!" Derek admitted freely. "She's a spoiled brat, and I love her, but she's got a long way to go before we get married."

Gem raised dark winged eyebrows. "You do plan to marry her, then?"

"Sure," Derek said easily. "I have since sixth grade."

"Does she have to meet some kind of test first?" Gem asked a little increduously.

To her surprise Derek considered the matter seriously. "I suppose so, in a way," he commented musingly. "If we got married now, we'd be divorced in a month."

"Why?" Gem was becoming more and more intrigued with this young man who seemed to know his own mind, yet did so without seeming arrogant.

Derek shrugged. "She's the only child of a rich family. She's had her own way from the time she was able to ask for what she wanted. In fact, she stopped asking a long time ago and started demanding." He gave her a wicked smile then. "I don't respond well to demands," he confided teasingly.

"Hmmm . . ." Gem considered him appraisingly, liking him more and more with each passing moment. "What's she demanding that you don't want to do?"

Derek's look grew more mature and somewhat brooding. "She wants me to go to work with an established architectural firm and keep her in the style to which she's become accustomed. Or better yet, she'd like me to let her father set me up on my own."

Gem thought about that for a while as they sat together in a companionable silence. "Don't do it," she said finally, her tone full of conviction. "You wouldn't like yourself if you did, and pretty soon you wouldn't like Sherri either."

Derek's grin was spontaneously delighted. "Right!" he said, placing an arm around her shoulders to give her a friendly squeeze. "I knew you were a girl after my own heart the moment I saw you."

Strangely Gem felt the same way. During the course of her talk with Derek she had begun to feel as though she had known him forever . . . that he was as close a friend as anyone she'd ever known before. She thought wonderingly how different he was from his brother and speculated how the difference had come to be.

"Derek . . ." Slowly she spoke her thought to him and was unembarrassed when he eyed her shrewdly.

"Roan's after you, isn't he?" he asked bluntly.

Gem shrugged. "Yes," she said, equally bluntly. "But I don't intend to give in to him. He's . . ." She gave a gesture of futility.

Derek finished the thought for her. "He's not interested in commitments, you mean?" he asked thoughtfully. "He's not the marrying kind?"

"Yes," Gem said in a defeated tone. "Why is that, Derek?" she asked in sad puzzlement. "You're not like that."

Derek gave a deep sigh and eyed her with wry resignation. "It's a long story," he said ruefully. "Do you feel like listening to a little family history?"

"Of course," Gem said with a faint smile. "In fact, I'm dying of curiosity, as you well know. Lead on, Macduff."

Derek chuckled, then grew serious again. "To understand Roan, you have to know what our father was like, Gem. He was a real rebel. In every way. He had his own rules and principles, and they didn't bear the slightest resemblance to most people's." Derek shrugged and shook his head in remembrance. "He led a most unorthodox life after our mom died. He lived like there was no tomorrow. He worked hard, he played hard, and"—here he eyed Gem with a cool speculativeness that matched his brother's —"he used up a lot of women in the process."

"Used them up?" Gem asked, her tone showing her puzzled repugnance.

Derek nodded. "We had one live-in surrogate mother after another, none of them interested in us, all of them fascinated by Dad. He took what he wanted from them until he got bored, then he got rid of them. That was the pattern Roan and I grew up with."

Gem felt chilled, the picture Derek drew of his father paralleling what she felt to be true of Roan. "And Roan is . . . ?" the half-question trailed off.

Derek nodded. "So far, he's followed the pattern. Oh, he's more respectable than Dad ever was in both his business dealings and in the way he handles his affairs with women. But he appears to be a chip off the old block, all right."

"How did you escape?" Gem asked after a moment of sad silence.

Derek grinned engagingly. "I didn't get my share of the Christianson fascination," he said with no regret, and at Gem's inquiring look he added, "It's true. The women spoiled Roan from the time he reached puberty. All he ever had to do was lift a hand, and one of them would come running. It's not surprising that he doesn't respect them, is it?"

Gem shook her head sadly, realizing she had done exactly as all the other women had on her first meeting with Roan. But that didn't mean she had to follow her first error with any further ones. Unconsciously she straightened her shoulders resolutely, and Derek noted the action.

"That's right," he said with quiet approval. "Hold firm, Gem, my girl. You may be the one who teaches him a lesson he badly needs to learn."

"I doubt it," Gem answered with sardonic fatalism. "I don't want to get close enough to him to get burned. I'll let someone else have the honor of teaching Roan Christianson that love means more than a willing bed partner." Then she added thoughtfully, "If he's capable of learning . . . which I doubt."

Derek took her hand in his and played with her fingers as he spoke with slow deliberation. "He's pretty nigh irresistible when he sets his mind to it, Gem. And I have the feeling he's set on having you."

A slight shudder shook Gem's slender body, and the hairs on her arms lifted slightly in warning. "We can't all have what we want," she responded more firmly than she felt.

"Maybe so," Derek said doubtfully. "But if you ask me, you need some protection."

Gem turned her head to look at him inquiringly. "Are you offering some?" she asked with rueful humor.

Derek surprised her by gazing back at her with serious thoughtfulness. "That might not be a bad idea," he mused. "If Derek loves anyone, it's me. Maybe he'd leave you alone if he thought the two of us were involved."

Gem looked at him askance. "What about Sherri?" she asked doubtfully. "You love her, remember?"

"Oh, I remember," Derek said with a touch of grimness. "But my patience is wearing a little thin where she's concerned. It might be that you could do me a favor by giving her a little pause for thought about what she's risking."

"Are you serious, Derek?" Gem asked, a frown drawing her brows together.

"Dead serious," Derek said with forceful vehemence, rising to his feet and bringing Gem up beside him. His eyes were alight with purpose now, and he bore the strongest resemblance to his brother Gem had yet seen. "How about it, Gem? Shall we help each other out?"

"Oh, Derek, I don't know . . ." Gem hesitated, feeling a little overwhelmed by Derek's suggestion. "If I try, I'm sure I can stay out of Roan's way."

Derek's laugh was not reassuring. "Don't kid yourself, babe," he said on a grim note. "You don't know him like I do. Once he sets his mind on something, he puts a bulldog to shame. I ought to know. It took everything I had to do what I wanted with my life instead of letting him run it. He wanted me in the business with him, and he still hasn't given up. I stay as far away from him as I can normally, though I love him. I just can't take the constant pressure. He hasn't given up on me yet." He eyed her consideringly. "If it's that hard for me to resist what he wants, what chance do you think you have? You aren't going to try to tell me he doesn't attract you, are you? The electricity sparks every time you look at each other."

Gem flushed at this revelation, but she didn't deny it

. . . she couldn't. Then she shook her head impatiently. "Derek, this is crazy. We've only just met tonight, and here we are plotting some elaborate scheme together. I think you're exaggerating about Roan. I have *some* willpower, after all, just as you do."

"Not enough, babe," Derek denied softly. "And I'm not exaggerating about Roan. He's never been denied anything he wanted for long before. He goes after it until he has it. It's that simple."

"He didn't get what he wanted from you," Gem held out stubbornly.

"He hasn't given up either," Derek said wryly. "And he loves me. He pulls his punches where I'm concerned."

"And he won't with me?" Gem asked somewhat bitterly.

"God, no!" Derek said vehemently. "With you he'll pull out all the stops." He lifted her chin with his hand and stared into her eyes with calm sympathy. "That's the way it is between men and women, honey. I plan to do exactly the same with Sherri."

Gem stared at him in disbelief for a moment before she accepted that he meant what he said. She realized he had his own share of the Christianson persistence and ruthlessness.

"All right," she capitulated angrily. "We'll see how it goes. But I'm not at all sure this is the right thing to do, Derek. I feel like running for cover instead of staying in Roan's vicinity."

Derek shook his head. "Never do that, babe." He grinned without humor. "The only way to win is to face up to the enemy. You know that's true, don't you?"

Gem refused to admit that she knew any such thing, but her capitulation was enough to satisfy Derek, it seemed. "Okay," he said with a deep breath of anticipation. "Let's get started. There's no time like the present, is there?"

From there on Derek took over, and before many moments had passed after they had rejoined the party, Gem was acutely conscious of two very different pairs of eyes piercing her with their hostile regard. Roan's expression made her quail inside, it was so ferocious. Sherri's was no less hostile, though tempered with a look of hurt that made Gem feel inordinately guilty at being a party to Derek's scheme to make the woman he loved jealous enough to allow him his own choice of career.

Jim Reasoner was the only one who seemed pleased about the seemingly spontaneous mutual attraction between Gem and Derek, but Gem would not have been happy had she known his real reason for such pleasure. Her father, recognizing Roan Christianson's competitive character as akin to his own, felt there was no harm in and perhaps a great deal to be gained by making the man he had decided was his daughter's match aware that he was going to have to work for her . . . perhaps the first time in his life he had faced such a situation.

Gem should have known she wasn't going to be allowed to escape a confrontation with Roan, but when it came, it took her by surprise. She was dancing with a friend of Derek's when Roan cut in, in a style calculated to intimidate the young man, who was more than happy to fill in for his friend on the dance floor with Gem.

The young man started to protest, but Roan shot him a look that threatened a lot more than a cold tone of voice, and the man drifted away hastily, unwilling to challenge the steel in Roan's manner.

"That was rude," Gem said between her teeth as Roan took her into his arms and started moving her at a brisk pace toward one end of the room.

"Was it?" Roan said stonily, obviously uncaring that he deserved such censure.

Before she was even aware she had a reason to protest, Roan had her off the dance floor and was steering her with a grip of iron toward the rear of the house. "Roan, stop it!" Gem protested as she became aware that here was the danger point she had faced all night. She had no doubt that Roan knew where his weapons lay, and that he wouldn't scruple to use every one of them. And she was full of doubts about her ability to defend herself.

"Shut up!" The barely suppressed violence in his tone was enough to cause Gem to do exactly as he'd ordered, and it was with compressed lips and storm in her eyes that Gem was guided into a small bedroom at the rear of Roan's home.

Once inside, Roan pushed her ahead of him, then turned back to lock the door behind him before facing her again where she stood rubbing the arm he had bruised in bringing her here.

"What do you want?" Gem asked with stony bravery.

"I've made it crystal clear what I want," Roan said with menace in his tone as he stalked her until her back was against the wall. "What the hell do you think you're doing playing with Derek?"

Gem faced him, her breathing ragged, her eyes wary as she hugged herself, ready to fend him off if he made any move to touch her. For the moment he seemed content to loom intimidatingly over her.

"I'm not *playing* with anyone, as you call it," Gem said disgustedly. "That's your department, remember?"

Roan nodded grimly. "And I play by my rules," he said, steel in his tone. "Stay away from him."

"No." Gem's defiance was dangerous, she knew, but Roan somehow was able to reduce her to the essentials . . . both physically and emotionally.

For a long moment Roan simply stared at her, his face seemingly graven in stone. Then, with a quickness that gave her no chance to maneuver, Roan's hands came up to grip her upper arms like a vise. "You want to live dangerously?" he questioned softly. "So be it."

His name was smothered on her lips as his mouth claimed her, branded her, drank the last dregs of her futile resistance. This was a new side of his lovemaking he hadn't shown her the night they'd met. Then he had held back, allowing her to find her balance before pushing her upward to another level of experience. This time she was subjected to the full enormity of his passion, and within seconds of his beginning his onslaught she had forgotten every shred of the resolve she had been struggling so hard to cement.

There was nothing in the world that mattered besides Roan's devouring mouth and her own response as she fought for every taste of him she could gain. He held her so tightly wrapped in his arms she felt her cells struggling to meld with his, and she moaned deep in her throat because the barrier of their clothing prevented that melding.

She felt wrapped in a shimmering, vividly explosive band of electricity that leaped from Roan's taut, straining body to her subjected one, and a cry of protest filled her throat as Roan turned her slightly with one powerful hand on her hip while he unleashed the tie that held her dress together.

A low, throaty growl came from between his lips as he heard that protest and interpreted it correctly, but that was his only verbal response to her dismay at losing bodily contact with him temporarily. Instead he pushed the filmy material back, exposing to his view and touch Gem's silken, swollen breasts. She trembled and bit her lip against a gasp as she felt the warmth of his palm and fingers begin to stroke what he had uncovered.

As Roan raised his head from his contemplation of the treasure he possessed to inspect with satisfaction the glaze of passion in Gem's storm-darkened eyes, he whispered with gruff arousal, "Do you really want Derek . . . or any other man for that matter . . . to touch you like this, Gem?"

An instinctive moan of denial parted her lips and had her shaking her head no before she caught herself up and closed her eyes to prevent the truth from blazing out at him. But it was too late. A soft, satisfied chuckle greeted her attempt to deceive him.

"You were never meant to deceive a man, Gem," he chided her with indulgent gentleness. "You were made to satisfy one." He then brushed one thumb lightly over one of her eyelids, causing her to open her eyes and blink at him with an expression of wary bemusement. He held her gaze, and his tone was softly inflexible as he added, "And I intend to be the one you satisfy.

I could take you right now, even with a hundred people, including your father, just down the hall, if I chose to."

The mention of her father stiffened Gem's resistance momentarily. She shook her head, knowing even as she spoke that her words were sheer bravado. "No . . . I wouldn't . . . I . . . "

Roan frowned as he shifted to grasp her shoulders and bring her up against him fully. "Grow up, Gem!" he muttered impatiently. "Stop fighting the inevitable! The kind of attraction we feel for each other doesn't come around every day, for God's sake! Aren't you woman enough yet to recognize that and take advantage of it when it happens?"

When Gem didn't answer but simply stared up at him with something akin to despair gathering in the clear luminescence of her eyes, Roan muttered a curse under his breath and lowered his head to taste the trembling vulnerability of Gem's mouth. "So sweet . . ." he grated huskily as he sipped the sweetness he spoke of. "So ripe . . ."

Gem felt the heat of him burning her own inflamed thighs as he stopped tasting and began to drink deeply of the sustenance he found within the warm interior of her erotically sensitized mouth. She felt the rough texture of his coat against the bare tautness of her breasts, and as he ravaged her defenses with his mouth and hands and lean, taut torso, she longed to take what he was offering with every fiber of her being.

When at last he granted her breath again, she found herself pleading, "Help me, Roan . . . please . . ." without knowing exactly what it was she was pleading for, his release or his possession.

"Oh, no." Roan's response was a growl between his teeth. "You *take* what you want, just as I'm going to do."

Inwardly Gem recoiled at the harshness of his decree that she accept and meet him halfway in this passion-filled embroilment between the two of them. She wanted tenderness, she wanted understanding, not just of her physical needs but of her emotional needs as well. And most of all she wanted him to hold out some hope that if she did as he asked and gave in to what both of them wanted, there could come to be more between them than an assuagement of sensual appetites.

Roan gave her no encouragement that such would be the case, however. He drew back and let his eyes roam her face and figure possessively, then he cupped her face with his hands and held her gaze.

"This is only the beginning," he promised with implacable purpose. "If you think I'm going to settle for less than everything the next time we meet, think again. I'm going to own you, body and soul, for as long as it takes to free us both from this obsession. You can count on it."

He straightened, still holding her eyes, before he smiled grimly, then turned on his heel and left the room.

Gem stared blindly at the closed door for long moments before she began to straighten her clothing with trembling fingers. Her thoughts were a jumble of wishes and wants and ingrained prohibitions against giving in to those wishes and wants.

She crossed to the mirror above the small dresser and stared at her troubled reflection, searching for answers to alleviate her conflicting desires, resenting the fact that the choices in life were not cut and dried with the promise of total satisfaction their reward. She had never dreamed she could want a man so badly as she wanted Roan Christianson until he had shown her her own passionate nature. And if she could have dreamed she would ever want a man so, she would not have believed she could want one without even loving him!

She still didn't believe it. Tilting her head in puzzlement, she stared into her own confused, cloudily bewildered gray eyes and asked herself the question she dreaded answering. Was she falling in love with Roan? A man who had made it clear that though he wanted her body, that was all he wanted? Or was she merely hiding behind that possibility in order to assuage guilt feelings at finding her body could overrule her principles at Roan's merest touch? And most important, was Roan as invincible as he seemed to be? If it turned out that she did love him, was there any remote possibility that her love could ignite his?

As Gem turned away to seek out her father and ask him to take her home, the only clear answer she had was that Roan would force the answers to her questions whether she wanted to know or not, and that was the only certainty to be had in the whole confusing, unwelcome maelstrom of emotion he had brought with him into her life.

CHAPTER EIGHT

Immediately the next morning Gem departed for the ranch, adamant against her father's ploys to keep her in Dallas. She needed to think, to gather her strength before Roan launched the next of his attacks in his campaign to make her his mistress.

She was quiet and withdrawn for three days after arriving, causing Rosita considerable concern that she might be coming down with an illness. She reassured her old friend as best she could, but she couldn't spare the energy to do a good job of it. She needed all she had to fight down the desire to run to Roan and beg for his possession again, knowing if she did so, she would shred her self-respect and give him a victory he hadn't earned and didn't deserve.

On the fourth day Derek called, and at the sound of his voice on the phone Gem thought for one heart-stopping moment that it was Roan. She sagged with relief when some nuance in the tones that were so similar to Roan's alerted her that this was Derek, and not the man who had the power to place her in the palm of his hand.

"Are you all right, Gem?" Derek asked, concern in his voice. "It's taken me three days to track you down. What happened when you disappeared with Roan the other night? He looked as grim as I've ever seen him when he came back, and I didn't see you come back at all."

"You don't want to know, Derek," Gem replied, gloom in her voice.

Derek was silent for a moment, taking in the implications in her words, before he said with genuine sympathy, "I'm sorry, kid. I didn't protect you very well, did I?"

Gem shrugged, forgetting for the moment that Derek couldn't see her. She was reflecting with puzzled curiosity on what reason Roan had had to look grim after he had left her that night. And then her eyes narrowed speculatively as she wondered if perhaps Roan was finding his attraction to her rather more than he had bargained for . . . perhaps greater than any he had ever felt for any woman before?

"Gem?" Derek's voice brought her back to the present.

"I'm sorry, Derek," she replied absently, her thoughts still on Roan. "What did you say?"

"I asked how you'd like to go to Midland with me," Derek replied with cheerful patience. "There's an experimental complex being built there that I helped design. Some magazine people are coming out to see it and interview the architects. I need some company for the long drive."

"What about Sherri?" Gem asked logically and then added more thoughtfully, "or is she mad at you because of the other night?"

"You've got it," Derek answered wryly. "She thinks if she denies me her company for a while, I'll come to heel."

"And will you?" Gem asked gently.

"No way," Derek asserted determinedly. "She can damned well sit home and sulk until she wakes up to the fact that it isn't going to get her her way." He paused then and added more quietly, "There is one thing you ought to know, though, Gem. Roan will be there. He's got business in the area, and though he disapproves of my work, he likes to keep tabs on what I'm doing. Do you think you're up to seeing him so soon?"

Gem didn't say what was on her mind, which was that it wouldn't matter whether it was one day or ten years before she saw Roan again. His effect on her would be the same. "It doesn't matter," she said to Derek, which was only the truth. "When are you going, Derek?"

"Tomorrow. I'd pick you up in the morning, and you'd need to bring clothes for a couple of days. It's a long drive."

Gem thought about it a second, then delayed her decision. "Can I think about it and call you back tonight, Derek?" she asked.

"Sure," he answered and gave her his number. "I'll understand if you decide not to, kid," he said sympathetically, "but like I told you before, running away is no answer."

"You may just be right, Derek," Gem answered with wry humor, "but right now I need a little time to think about that."

They rang off, and Gem strolled restlessly toward the back of the house, letting herself out onto the back patio, where she dropped into a chaise longue by the pool to gaze sightlessly at the rolling hills of pasture stretching out to the horizon. She lost track of time as she contemplated her choices with the equanimity of one whose maturity was being forced to grow by leaps and bounds under the influence of Roan Christianson. There was no middle ground. She could either run or end up Roan's mistress. And running didn't appeal to her. Not nearly so much as the opportunity to love Roan did.

She let her eyes close as she thought about the consequences of becoming Roan's mistress. How long would it take him to grow bored with her? And did he necessarily *have* to grow bored with her? Wasn't he showing signs that she affected him as strongly as he affected her? And that the fact disturbed him? He had said that the attraction they felt for one another didn't come along every day. He had even referred to it as an "obsession." She had the distinct impression Roan Christianson had never labored under such an obsession before, and surely that was something to build upon, wasn't it?

"Gem?" The soft, masculine voice with Spanish overtones interrupted her thoughts and caused her to sit up with a jerk.

"Pedro?" Gem turned disbelieving, joyous eyes on the slight form of the man who approached her, his deep velvet eyes caressing her with a devotion she had always had from him and knew she would never lose. "Pedro!" she said again, jumping to her feet to throw herself into his arms. "You're home!"

"Yes, and it is good to be so," Pedro responded with laughter as Gem kissed and hugged him fervently. He returned her lavish caresses before he held her off to look at her. "Mamma has told me your good news," he said with deep pride in her accomplishment. "I knew it would be so. Didn't I always tell you that?"

"Yes, you always did, Pedro," Gem said with loving affection, linking her arm with his and drawing him down onto the chaise longue with her. "But, then, you were always prejudiced, and I took your predictions with a grain of salt."

Pedro fixed her with a mock scowl. "Do not use such a word to a Spanish-American, Gem," he scolded her piously. "You know we are not tainted with such an unthinkable trait."

Gem threw back her head and laughed, feeling comforted, warmed, and content, as she always had with Pedro since the time they were barefooted children causing Rosita to clutch her hair in despair twenty times a day at their antics. "Of course not," she said, returning his mockery with interest. "We all know you are the salt of the earth." But for all her teasing she believed profoundly in the truth of what she said, at least in Pedro and Rosita's case. They were gold in a world of tinsel, and for one brief moment Gem wondered what metal would describe Roan—iron or steel? Or something more fragile where the right woman was concerned?

"How is your practice going?" she asked Pedro, shaking off her thoughts of Roan momentarily. "Do you like the town where you're working?"

"Like?" Pedro's deep-set, depthless eyes took on a faraway look. "No, I cannot say I like the town," he admitted truthfully. "It is a hellhole, nothing less. But the people . . ." He shrugged and smiled his sweet smile. "They are beautiful, yes."

They fell into a companionable silence as Gem reflected on the gentle selflessness of the man beside her. He had always been a healer, starting even as a small boy to bring home small animals in need of care. Her father had recognized his talent and seen to it that his schooling was of the best, even to the point of sending him to medical school. Now Pedro had dedicated his life to helping those of his race who were unlikely to get quality medical care from anyone else, though it meant he must live in the "hellhole" he had described, far from the luxury he had grown up in. Though he and Rosita were paid employees of the Reasoners, they had never been treated as such, but rather as family. And in their turn the Reasoners had been rewarded with a devotion and loyalty and love that Gem thought would be hard to match anywhere.

Unconsciously she toyed with the necklace she wore always as she thought of Pedro and his mother, until she noticed Pedro's eyes on it and smiled her love to him. "Yes, it's still my good luck charm, Pedro. I wouldn't be without it. Now, tell me. Have you found someone else you would be willing to work your fingers to the bone for in order to buy her a trinket such as this?"

Pedro smiled gently and nodded. "Yes," he answered with the simplicity that was the most appealing of his many sterling qualities. "And the trinket this time will be a wedding ring, I think."

"Oh, Pedro, that's wonderful!" Gem cried, her joy in his happiness as complete as though it were her own. "Did you bring her with you so we can meet her?"

He shook his dark head chidingly. "Not this time, Gem. She is Spanish, and there was no one to escort her here and act as chaperon for her. I will bring her when I can, though it will not be until we are married, perhaps."

Gem was indignant. "What do you mean, after you're married! Don't you plan to invite us to the wedding?"

Pedro looked at her very seriously. "It will be nothing fancy, you realize, Gem. Her people cannot afford much."

For the first time since she'd known him, Gem was truly angry at her beloved Pedro. "And what is that supposed to mean?" she demanded heatedly. "That we'd be too good to come to a *simple* wedding?"

Pedro took her hands into his own, his dark eyes chiding her for her temper. "It is not you I am concerned with, Gem," he said gently. "It is her people. Do you not think it might embarrass them to have you visit them in their humble home?"

Gem stared at him, her temper still unabated. "Then they are snobs, Pedro," she stated firmly. "And you shouldn't marry into a family of snobs!"

For a moment Pedro looked taken aback by her characterization of his humble prospective in-laws as snobs, but then he caught her meaning, and his laughter was rich and full. When he was able to speak again, he conceded defeat. "All right, all right," he protested as Gem pummeled him playfully with her fists. "You can come, if it is that important to you. But you will *not,* you understand, give elaborate gifts. That would be too much!"

Gem shrugged, refusing to agree to any such thing. "You let me be the judge of what I want to give as a wedding gift, Pedro Ramirez," she sniffed disdainfully. "It isn't proper to specify what you want."

Pedro shook his head at her turning the tables on him again, then caught her hand to pull her to her feet. "Well, now that we've got that settled, let's go see if we can get Mamma to give us something to eat. I'm starving to death!"

Laughing, their arms around each other's waists, the two of them made the journey once again to plead for food from Pedro's mother and Gem's surrogate mother, as they had done countless times in the past, confident that despite her protestations Rosita would come through for them as she always had, stuffing them so full they couldn't move.

And later, as they caught up on each other's news in detail, Gem finally gave in to the perceptive, curious looks Pedro had been giving her all evening and approached the subject she was longing to discuss with him but had been too afraid to broach. She relaxed as she remembered that, although straitlaced himself, Pedro had never been anything but understanding of those foibles most of the human race displayed from time to time.

"What is it, Gem?" Pedro coaxed gently as he saw her eyeing

him hesitantly. "You have had something on your mind all evening. You know you can tell me anything, don't you?"

Gem sighed, then nodded in relief. "Yes, I know, Pedro. It's just that it's a difficult thing to tell."

"Ah, then it concerns a man," Pedro stated confidently, then laughed as Gem gave him a mock scowl. "Why so nervous, *pequeña?* It is about time you became involved with someone, isn't it? You are too beautiful and loving to remain untouched forever."

Gem bit her lip and eyed Pedro warily at the way he had phrased his statement, causing him to raise his dark eyebrows knowingly. "I see," he said softly. "You have *not* remained untouched, then."

Taking a deep breath, Gem shook her head. "You're right, Pedro," she said ruefully. "I think I can safely say I have not remained untouched."

And then she poured out the story of her relationship with Roan to date, ending with the dilemma she now faced. As she raised her eyes to Pedro's dark, sympathetic gaze, she pleaded, "What would you do if you were me, Pedro? Take the chance that this attraction Roan and I have for each other could develop into something more, even though he's not interested in marriage? Or avoid him . . . and possibly a lot of pain in the process?"

Pedro got up to come and sit beside her, placing a comforting arm around her shoulders. "No one can answer that question for you, Gem," he said in his slow, soft, accented voice. "But perhaps I can help you find your own answer." He shifted so that he could look into her eyes. "If you manage to avoid him—which I somehow think, from what you have told me about this Roan, may prove to be impossible—will you be able to forget him? Will you not always wonder what it could have been like? Will you have regrets in the years to come that you refused to take the chance and find out what could develop?"

Gem thought that over for a while, and when her answer came, it was firm. "Oh, yes, Pedro," she said softly. "I have no doubt that I would regret running away. I'm already half in love with him, you see."

"I see that clearly every time you speak his name," Pedro said calmly.

"You do?" Gem asked rather dazedly. "It's that obvious?"

Pedro gave a short laugh and a shrug. "It's that obvious," he assured her. "And though I said I couldn't answer your question for you, I will tell you what I feel. I think it might be best for you to explore the possibilities with this Roan. It's possible to do that today, whereas it wouldn't have been in the past. Perhaps with this particular man it will not be possible to say good-bye to him until you have said hello to him fully and given yourself an opportunity to either make the relationship work or get him out of your system once and for all."

He smiled a rather sheepish smile and then, as he saw Gem looking at him in surprise, said, "Oh, I know this must seem strange advice coming from me, but I am learning there are not always clear-cut rules for everyone." He frowned then and looked down at her in mock fear. "But I hope you will not tell your papa about this advice I have given you. Somehow I do not think he would appreciate it at all!"

Gem laughed and shook her head to reassure him. "No, I won't tell Daddy, Pedro." She sobered then and looked uneasy. "If I give in to Roan, it will be enough of a blow to Daddy without his feeling you let him down too."

Pedro frowned and looked hurt. "I do not think of it as letting Jim down, Gem. I would never do anything against the man who has given me so much."

"I know, Pedro," Gem hastened to reassure him. "I didn't mean it like that. It's just that Daddy is so old-fashioned and so protective of me . . ." She sighed, feeling torn between her loyalty to her father and her own desire to experience what Roan had to offer.

Rosita came in then, obviously wanting to visit with her son in private for a while, and Gem felt guilty at monopolizing him. "No, no, *niña,*" Rosita scolded her. "I have been busy. But now you have had your turn with Pedro"—she grinned engagingly—"and I want him back. We have to talk about the wedding, no?" She beamed, obviously ecstatic at the prospect.

"Yes!" Gem laughed, pushing Pedro toward his mother. He turned back for an instant, his eyes asking a question. "Thank you, Pedro," she said softly, grateful for his concern. "I'll let you know what I decide."

He nodded, then wrapped an arm around his mother's shoulders, bending his dark head down with indulgent fondness to listen to her questions about her future daughter-in-law and his prospective in-laws and the wedding.

Gem watched them go, wishing a little forlornly that things could work out so satisfactorily for herself. Then she got up to wander to the patio doors and gaze out into the soft blackness of the night. After a while she firmed her shoulders, and there was a distinct light of anticipatory challenge in her gray eyes as she turned to find the telephone and call Derek to tell him she would be happy to accompany him to Midland . and to Roan

CHAPTER NINE

During the long drive to Midland, Gem and Derek cemented their new friendship to a point where they felt free to discuss almost anything that came to mind. In keeping with that relaxed intimacy Gem asked a question that had been niggling at her mind.

"Derek . . ." She brought him back from some daydream—perhaps of Sherri?—and his tone was abstracted when he acknowledged her.

"Why is it Sherri feels you need more money? Is everything Roan's?"

"Yep. He made it. It's all his."

"But wasn't it your father's business he started with?"

Derek snorted. "If you could call it a business," he agreed. "But it was on its last legs before Roan took over. No"—he shook his head firmly—"that business is what Roan made it. I have no claim to it, and I wouldn't want it if I did."

"And Roan won't help you because he doesn't like your choice of career?" Gem persisted.

"Help?" Derek looked puzzled for a second, then frowned, glancing down at Gem in disapproval. "You mean start me up in a firm of my own?" And at Gem's sheepish nod he glared at her. "And what would be the difference between accepting that from him and accepting it from Sherri's father? I thought you understood I wanted to make it on my own."

"I do, Derek," Gem said in an apologetic tone. "I'm sorry. For a moment there I forgot what it's like to be smothered by someone else's success."

"Your dad?" Derek asked with a grin.

Gem nodded. "Yes. I love him dearly, and he doesn't understand why I won't just let him support me. But it's different when you make your own success, isn't it?"

Derek laughed. "I hope so. Ask me that when I *become* a success!"

Gem scoffed at his modesty. "I suppose those magazine people are coming to see your work because they like to feature failures?" she asked mockingly.

With a shrug Derek accepted only his fair share of the praise. "I'm only one of a group of architects who are working on this project, Gem. This doesn't mean I've made it yet."

"Well, it's a start," Gem defended him loyally. "It could lead to other things, too, right?"

"Right," Derek answered with satisfaction at the prospect.

As they neared their destination Gem began to feel a combination of dread and excitement at the thought of seeing Roan again. "Does Roan know I'm coming?" she asked, trying to sound casual.

Derek shot her a perceptive look and reached down to squeeze one of her hands. "No," he said calmly. "He hasn't been in town the past few days." Then he shot her a wicked grin. "You want to make a bet he won't be pleased when he finds out?" And at Gem's rather startled look he explained what he meant. "Oh, I don't mean that he won't be glad to see you. It's just that I don't think he'll like the fact that you came here with *me.*"

"Oh," Gem said rather faintly, remembering with uneasy clarity how Roan had reacted the last time he had thought she was making a play for Derek. "Well," she said with a nonchalant shrug, "we're both adults. What can he do about it?"

But Derek's wry ruefulness matched her own sense of caution. "Short of punching me out and kidnaping you, I don't know," he teased, but then he looked at her seriously. "But I need to know before we get there just how far you want my protection to extend. I have the distinct impression you wouldn't have come with me today if you hadn't known Roan was going to be here too."

Gem flushed a little at that but decided that Derek deserved her honesty. "I . . . I do want to see him again, Derek," she admitted. "I think you're right about running away not being the answer. But I still have some thinking to do about how far I want to get involved with him."

Derek lifted an eyebrow, his expression sardonic. "In other words you want us to play it by ear," he suggested. And at Gem's nod he shook his head slightly. "You're playing with fire, girl," he advised her. "But like you said, you're an adult, and you'll have to make your own decisions. I just hope . . ." He let the thought trail off, but Gem knew he had been going to say that he hoped Roan didn't break her heart. And as they approached the building site and she saw Roan climbing out of his car, the sight of his tall, lithe frame made her breath catch in her throat, and she found herself hoping the same thing.

Derek's sly chuckle made her turn to him, and he shot her a wicked look from dancing eyes. "Roan might win in the end, but we don't have to make it easy for him, do we?" he asked with mischievous purpose.

Gem looked at him uneasily. "No, I don't want to make it easy for him, Derek, but I don't want to cause any trouble between the two of you, either," she said firmly, then added, "At least not *serious* trouble."

Derek laughed confidently as he pulled to a stop near where Roan stood waiting. "Leave it to me, kid," he said insouciantly. "I've had a lot of years to learn just how far to push my big brother."

Gem hoped he was right, but she had the feeling he might not be when she caught sight of Roan's grim face as he approached the car on Derek's side and leaned down to speak to his brother through the window.

"Derek . . ." Roan nodded his head at his brother. "I was beginning to wonder if you were going to make it at all, but I see you had reason to be delayed." His cold tone failed to move Derek.

"Hi, big brother," he greeted Roan cheerfully. "Yep, I wanted Gem to see my work, and I'm delighted to say she was *happy* to come." Derek's deliberate exaggeration brought an even grimmer expression to Roan's hard face, and Derek hid a grin as he saw a telltale muscle twitch in his brother's jaw.

Roan then turned his attention to Gem. "Hello, Gem. I've been looking forward to seeing you again." The low intimacy in his voice was both a threat and a promise, and Gem remembered all too clearly what Roan had promised would happen the next time they met. She swallowed down her mingled alarm and anticipation as she nodded coolly at him.

She and Derek climbed out of the car, and Gem was startled when Derek practically raced Roan to get to her side first. He took her hand in his and smiled down at her warmly, but when Gem saw Roan's expression as he watched the two of them, she wanted to drop Derek's hand like a hot poker. Instead she gave Derek a warm smile in her turn, but her eyes pleaded with him to *be careful.*

For Derek's sake Gem wished she could have paid more attention to his prideful tour of the building project. But she saw its stark, modernistic lines through a blur and heard his enthusiastic words through a haze of awareness of Roan. Derek paid her no small amount of attention, covering for her when she didn't hear him, touching her with an ease and familiarity that she knew, even without looking at him, infuriated Roan.

He grew more and more silent as the tour progressed, and his silence was more eloquent than a thrown glove of challenge would have been. Even Derek began to look concerned as he surreptitiously watched his brother's reaction to their little charade. He began to wonder seriously at the extent of Roan's feelings for Gem, hoping against all reason that his beloved brother had at last found the woman who would teach him to love.

But there was no love in Roan's voice when he spoke to Gem

at last. "How long will you be here?" he demanded abruptly, paying no notice to both Derek and Gem's arrested stillness at the tone of his question.

For the first time Gem lifted her gray eyes to Roan's coldly angry brown ones, and she had to swallow before she could speak. "Until tomorrow afternoon, I believe. Is that right, Derek?"

"That's right." Derek injected hearty cheerfulness into his reply, though in truth he was getting a little nervous about the whole situation. "We've got rooms in Midland for the night, Roan. When are you leaving? This afternoon?"

Roan's stance had all the dangerousness of a panther relaxing before his strike. "No," he drawled, his eyes never leaving Gem, "I'm staying over too." He then inquired in a clipped voice where the two of them had reservations, and with an abrupt turn he strode to his car without even bothering to say good-bye.

When he was out of earshot, Derek rolled his eyes heavenward. "Whew!" he breathed with relief. "I haven't seen him that mad in a long, long time!"

Gem shifted nervously and eyed Derek warily. "I thought you said you knew how far to push him!" she accused.

Derek grinned rather sheepishly, then looked at Gem with thoughtful speculation. "I thought I did, too, but we've never tangled over a woman before. In fact, I've never known Roan to tangle with *anyone* over a woman before. I don't think he's ever had to, or that he ever cared enough to go to the trouble, even if he did face a little competition."

A little frisson of pleasure chased Gem's spine at that information, followed by a shiver of alarm. She was beginning to have a strong sense of inevitability about what was going to happen between her and Roan, and she still wasn't certain she was being wise in allowing things to escalate so precipitously.

After they finished the tour of the building site, they drove into Midland for dinner and to check into their motel rooms. All evening Gem was in a state of tense excitement as she waited for Roan to put in an appearance, and by the time it became apparent that he wasn't going to show up, she felt drained and exhausted by her emotional tension.

Feeling cross and unaccountably let down, she showered and donned a filmy nightgown before crawling between the crisp, clean sheets of her bed, certain she wouldn't be able to sleep. She was so tired, however, that she did sleep almost immediately, and she had no way of knowing how much time had passed before a persistent knock on her door roused her and brought her up frowning groggily at the offending noise. When the knock came again, she dragged herself out of bed to stagger across the room and lean wearily against the wall beside the door. "Who is it?" she asked in a cross voice muffled by sleep.

"Derek," came the soft reply, and with a frown of annoyance Gem reached up to fumble with the chain before swinging the door open a mere two inches.

"Derek, what—" Her words were cut off as the door swung violently inward and Roan strode across the threshhold with all the suppressed, taut energy of a charging bull. He reached out to slam the door closed behind him as Gem stepped back, her eyes wide and anxious as she took in the anger in every line of Roan's rugged face and body. She saw him rake the bed with his eyes, then turn back to her with a scowl.

"You and Derek haven't gotten to the bedroom stage yet, I see," he drawled with hard sarcasm. "Though perhaps I just got here too early? You were certainly quick enough to open the door when you thought it was him."

Angered in her turn, Gem placed a hand on her hip and adopted a challenging stance. "I don't know, what time is it?" she questioned scathingly, glaring back at him. She had left the bathroom light on, and now she reached behind her and flipped the switch by the door up, flooding the room with light. Then she deliberately raised her arm to glance at her watch. "Ah, I see it's only three A.M.," she purred sarcastically. "Derek should be here any minute now. He enjoys waking me from a sound sleep before he makes love—"

She couldn't finish as Roan's hand shot out to enclose her

wrist in an iron-hard grip. "Be quiet!" he rasped as he jerked her to him, folding her arm behind her as he raised her face to his with the other hand. "I'm in no mood for your games tonight!"

"Games!" Gem struggled to put scorn in her voice, though her body was already reacting in a totally predictable fashion. "I'm not the one who plays games, remember?"

"Nor do I!" Roan growled as he forced her closer to him. "Not this time. This has gone on long enough. You're mine, and from now on no one's going to be left in any doubt about it, least of all you!" He caught her mouth in a bruising kiss then, but as he felt Gem's wince he softened the kiss to a hungry, more gentle attack.

After a moment, with a muffled groan, he lifted his head and pulled her to the bed, where he stripped the nightgown from her in one deft motion, then lifted her off her feet to lay her down. Straightening, he began to remove his own clothing while his eyes concentrated on devouring the feast before his eyes.

"Roan . . ." Gem faltered, her desire warring with her common sense. "Wait . . . we need to talk . . ." She didn't know whether she was glad or sorry when he shook his head determinedly.

"Do you think I wouldn't stop if I could, my reluctant little temptress?" he said in a tone of self-mockery she would never have expected to hear from him. "I don't want this involvement between us any more than you do, but I can't think of any way to get you out of my system other than to immerse myself completely for a while." He paused before moving slowly toward her. "And that's exactly what I plan to do," he said very softly before lowering himself beside her onto the bed.

Gem watched him as he loomed over her, her heart beginning to beat frantically with excitement. Her doubts were somehow calmed at realizing Roan was in the grip of the same powerful force that held her captive. She let her qualms slip away from her as he began to touch her, his palm warm and excitingly masculine as it skimmed her skin. There was no resisting him, and she didn't even want to try anymore.

She waited, almost breathless, for his mouth to descend upon hers and begin the spiral that would take them to the heights together once again. Then she saw him pause, his eyes growing cool as they focused on the necklace Pedro had given her, which she wore even to bed.

"Who gave you that?" he gritted out harshly.

Gem thought it might be safer to lie but was unable to do so under the powerful force of Roan's gaze and personality. "Pedro . . ." she admitted in a husky whisper.

She saw his jaw tighten and his mouth firm into a hard line. "Take it off!" he demanded quietly, but the force of that demand left her feeling shaken inside. She raised her hands toward her throat, then faltered, feeling bereft at the thought of disposing of her long-treasured pendant.

With a murmured growl of impatience Roan did it for her, not bothering to unclasp the chain but merely giving a powerful yank that stung her skin as the links broke apart. "Roan . . ." Gem protested.

He replaced the chain with his hand, circling her throat with the warm strength of his fingers and rubbing away the hurt. "I'm sorry if I hurt you," he said in a low voice. "But while you're mine I don't want you wearing gifts from other men, understand?"

"Yes, Roan," Gem whispered, and she did. The raw possessiveness blazing at her from Roan's tawny eyes made it very clear to her, thrilling her and bringing a slight apprehensiveness at the same time. She closed her eyes against it, waiting for Roan to begin to love her.

"Look at me," he ordered softly, and as Gem's eyes fluttered open to reveal her growing passion, he murmured, "That's better. Kiss me, Gem. This thing between us is mutual. I want you to acknowledge that."

Slowly Gem raised her palms to his face and drew his head down to hers until she could reach his lips. And when she touched the magnetism of his mouth, something inside her relaxed while something else began to flicker into flame. As had happened before on the night when Roan had first made love to her, she reacted with total spontaneity, feeling as though she had always belonged to him, with not even the slightest sense of strangeness that she could be so free in her loving with a man who, even now, she barely knew.

Her commitment to the gamble Roan represented became cemented in that night of passion, on some deep level beneath conscious thought. Her body knew him, as his seemed to know hers. Could she do less than grant the two of them the time, the intimacy they needed to allow their minds and hearts to catch up with what their primal selves already knew?

CHAPTER TEN

Gem woke the next morning to find Roan staring down at her, his head propped on one hand, his expression brooding and almost resentful. A small gasp escaped her lips at rousing to find herself the object of that enigmatic gaze, but when it softened to a sensuous, possessive inspection, her alarm turned to a hesitant smile.

"Good morning, Roan," she said softly, her confusion at how to approach him on this momentous morning evident in her tone.

"You sleep like a child," was his low-voiced greeting. "Oblivious, completely relaxed, and innocent. Do you always sleep that hard, or were you exceptionally tired?" There was a teasing suggestion in his voice that made the color rise gently in Gem's silken cheeks.

"You know I was tired, Roan," she chided quietly. "You didn't allow me to sleep at all until very late, remember?"

His smile started now familiar fires beneath Gem's outwardly calm, sleepily hazy gray eyes. "I remember," he murmured, and she heard the male satisfaction in his voice and responded to it. "Kiss me, Gem. I want to see if you taste as good as you look in the morning."

Slightly amused at Roan's insistence that she carry her share of the responsibility for what was happening between them but unable to resist his quiet instruction, Gem raised her tousled head slightly to meet his lips, secretly delighted that he was actually meeting her halfway, perhaps without realizing it.

The meeting was soft, explorative, tentative for long moments before with a low groan Roan gathered her closer to him and deepened the kiss, shuddering slightly as Gem smoothly accommodated her curves to the taut planes of his body. He drew back to give her a heavy-lidded look with passion-softened brown eyes. "You enchantress," he said thickly. "Where did you learn to melt into a man like that?"

"You taught me, Roan," Gem whispered shakily. "There's nothing I do my body didn't learn from yours."

"I was right, then?" he growled with satisfaction. "You are inexperienced?" And at Gem's weak nod he shook his head almost disbelievingly. "You learn exceptionally well . . . and exceptionally fast."

Gem's lower lip drooped enticingly as she looked at him with resigned reproach. "No," she denied with a sigh. "You *teach* exceptionally well . . . and *much* too fast." And as Roan didn't soften as a result of her mild reproach, she added, "Or perhaps it's just that our bodies know one another. How else do we explain what's happening against both our wills?"

Roan frowned then, releasing her to roll over on his back and stare up at the ceiling, his jaw tensed, the muscles rippling under the skin. "Yes," he drawled finally with a hard inflection. "There is that possibility if one believes in romantic nonsense." He failed to see the wounded flinch Gem gave involuntarily. "For my part I prefer my first explanation."

He turned to her then, his expression inflexible. "It doesn't matter why this has happened," he said hoarsely. "The important thing is to get over it." And on seeing the hurt in Gem's large eyes he made an impatient movement. "Grow up, Gem," he commanded. "I don't believe in marriage. That's not where this is heading. It won't last. Nothing this . . ." He searched for a word and failed to find it, then shrugged. "We'll take what we've got to offer each other, enjoy it, then go our separate ways. Don't count on anything else, understand?"

Gem lowered her gaze from him, holding back the tears that were moistening her long, black lashes. "I understand, Roan," she managed to get out levelly. "But you don't," she couldn't help adding with a surge of resentment. "I *do* believe in marriage, and in love and commitment and loyalty. Call it romantic nonsense if you want to," she burst out angrily at seeing his closed expression. "But it's there to be had between people who aren't ruined for life by—"

She broke off at the anger she saw rising in Roan's now hard brown eyes. "Has Derek been telling you about our poor misguided childhood?" he said mockingly. "I wouldn't take all of that too seriously if I were you. I live in the here and now, not in the past."

Gem started to say something about how the past could affect one for his entire life, then fell silent as she realized anything she had to say on that subject would fall on deaf ears. Instead she shrugged in defeat and made a move to get up, unwilling to remain close to Roan for the moment.

"Where are you going?" he demanded, crossing a powerful arm over her to keep her where she was.

"I . . . I wanted to take a shower and get dressed. It's getting late," Gem faltered, not wanting to explain the gulf between them as a result of his words.

"Can it wait a moment?" Roan said more quietly. "We need to make plans."

"Plans?" Gem asked dully. "I thought we just did."

"Generally, yes. Specifically, no." Roan raised a hand to turn her head to his, frowning slightly at the moisture he saw in Gem's eyes but refusing to comment on it. "I want you to live with me for a while."

Gem went still for an instant, then relaxed. She hadn't really thought before about *how* they would conduct this affair, merely that they would. But actually living with Roan presented some problems she knew would be hurtful. "My father . . ." she murmured abstractedly, her tone sad.

Roan's look was impatiently male. "Are you still such a child that you worry about your father's reaction to your love life, Gem? He's a man of the world."

"Not where I'm concerned, he isn't," Gem muttered. "It will hurt him terribly." She chewed her swollen lower lip in agitation as she spoke her thoughts aloud. "I don't want to lose his respect."

"Good God, woman!" Roan exclaimed. "What does it have to do with losing respect? We're adults. If we choose to live this way rather than soothing society by getting married and then divorced, isn't it more honest and a hell of a lot less trouble to do it this way? Hell, I've never even asked a woman to live with me before!" He spoke as though that fact should impress her, and Gem's eyes turned to cool slate as she gazed up at him.

"Am I supposed to be *honored* by that fact?" she asked with mild sarcasm. "Should I feel special because the great Roan Christianson has decided I'm sufficiently enticing to allow into his home?" She gave a grimace and added dryly, "However *temporarily.*"

Roan's eyes narrowed, and his face took on the expression she was coming to know meant he was intent on having his way. Gem regarded that expression with resignation, already well acquainted with Roan's success at getting what he set his mind on.

"Sarcasm doesn't suit you, honey," he drawled calmly, and then he raised a finger to trace her lips lingeringly. "What's it to be?" he murmured as Gem's mouth involuntarily parted at his touch. "Will you live with me? Don't you want to?"

Gem didn't answer for a moment, her gaze searching Roan's for something she knew it was too soon to find. Was he right? she wondered a little forlornly. Was their mutual passion too intense to last? And when the heat diminished, would they be left with anything worthwhile to keep them together? Roan thought not. She hoped so. But whichever of them turned out to be right, she knew she would no longer run away from finding the answer.

"For how long, Roan?" she asked huskily, her tone displaying her acceptance.

"For as long as it takes," Roan replied, a slight resentment in his tone which Gem instinctively knew sprang from his irritation at finding himself so attracted to a woman, he could not accept letting her go . . . at least not yet. He gave a dry laugh as he swung his powerful body away from her and got to his feet. "You can pray it won't take long, little coward. It never has in the past."

He flexed his muscles in an impatient movement and headed toward the bathroom. "I'll shower first if you want to rest awhile longer," he said, and then as he noted her eyes on him he flashed her a self-confident grin. "Unless you want to join me and wash my back?" he asked softly, pausing to face her with his hands on his hips, as unselfconscious in his nudity as any Greek god and just as masculinely appealing.

Gem gave a negative shake of her head, though it cost her to refuse what he offered. She was feeling slightly guilty at the greed he inspired in her and wanted to assert her willpower, even if only in this small way.

As if he understood her thoughts, Roan grinned again, shook his head at her chidingly, and continued on his way. "That won't last long, honey," he said with complete assurance. "But if it comforts you, enjoy it while it lasts." And then he was gone, leaving Gem scowling at his taunt.

By the time it was Gem's turn to shower, she had gained some control over her emotions, but later, as she came out of the bathroom wrapped in a fluffy white towel to see Roan finishing a phone call, there came a knock on the door that froze her where she stood. It could only be Derek, and one look at Roan's tight smile told her he didn't intend to spare her any embarrassment in the forthcoming encounter.

"You might as well get used to it, Gem," he said, mocking her panicky expression. "It will be common knowledge soon enough."

He got to his feet and approached the door while Gem, unable to face Derek just yet, fled back into the bathroom to the sound of Roan's mocking chuckle. She slammed the door behind her even as she heard Roan's deep voice greeting his brother.

For long moments she stood with her back pressed against the bathroom door, her eyes closed, listening to the muffled sound of voices that began to grow in volume. Then she jumped as she heard a knock on the panel of the door directly behind her back. "Come out, Gem," Roan said in a terse command. "Derek wants to see that you're all right." The mockery in his voice was clearly audible, and Gem bit her lip in pain at the sound. Then she opened her eyes to see her white, drawn face in the mirror across from the door, her huge gray eyes rounded and staring while she made her decision. A sense of calm invaded her as she faced exactly what Roan Christianson's advent into her life was going to mean to her pride . . . faced it and accepted it and turned to throw open the door and greet it.

Derek's eyes widened as she came through the door still wrapped in her white towel, her face composed and regal, her eyes calmly meeting his, though there was a slight appeal for understanding in their depths.

"Good morning, Derek," she said with quiet calm.

"Gem!" Derek's eyes roamed over her, focusing on a small bruise on her throat. "Are you all right?" he asked grimly, his eyes snapping to his older brother, who stood lounging easily with his arms crossed, though his brown eyes were alert and ready for anything.

Gem nodded her head, looking like a queen acknowledging a subject, though she wasn't feeling very queenly at the moment. "I'm fine, Derek. Roan hasn't . . . hasn't hurt me." The lie stuck in her throat, though it was true Roan hadn't hurt her physically; only her emotions had been damaged and might continue to be by her ill-fated obsession with the man who was compelling her to undertake a very dangerous gamble.

Derek compressed his lips, looking frustrated and angry, yet unable to think of what he could do to help Gem. In his anger he turned on Roan. "Damn it, Roan, why can't you leave her alone?"

One dark eyebrow arched upward as Roan eyed his brother sardonically and then turned to Gem. "Do you want me to leave you alone, Gem?" he asked politely, his eyes raking her from head to foot, kindling fire in her wherever they touched.

Unable to speak, Gem swallowed, then gave a bare shake of her head in the negative. Upon seeing this Derek's eyes shone with frustration and sympathy. "Are you about ready to leave, Gem?" he said, changing the subject and giving her an out at the same time.

"Gem won't be leaving with you, Derek." Roan stepped close to Gem and wrapped a leisurely arm around her shoulders. "She's coming back with me in the plane . . . to my house."

Gem closed her eyes against the disappointment in Derek's. "Is that true, Gem?" Derek asked gruffly.

In the long second that followed, Gem felt Roan's hand tighten on her shoulder, and the contact, however temporary and however destructive to her principles, gave her strength. She opened her eyes and faced Derek squarely. "Yes, Derek. I'm going to be living with Roan . . . for a while." The last was said on a note of hopeful hesitancy, but if either man heard it, neither reacted to it.

Derek relaxed, though his expression was sad for her. "Ah, Gem," he commiserated. "You couldn't . . ."

She shook her head hard. "No, Derek, I couldn't," she asserted, spelling out her inability to resist what was, and might come to be, between her and Roan.

A hard line came to Derek's jaw as he faced his brother. "Damn it, Roan . . ." he started to argue, but Roan cut him off.

"Stay out of this, little brother," he ordered. "It's nothing to do with you. Gem's a grown woman, and I'm a grown man. And anyone who gets between a man and his woman tends to get hurt. I'm too fond of you to see that happen."

The brothers' eyes warred for a moment before Derek accepted the inevitability of the situation. Finally he turned his gaze to Gem, and the soft brown was supportive and affectionate. "If he hurts you, he'll answer to me," he promised in a tone that matched his brother's at its most inflexible.

Gem smiled waveringly, gratefully at her would-be protector, wondering if he realized his brother's brand of hurt could be invisible and everlasting. "Thank you, Derek," she whispered.

"I'll no doubt answer to a lot of people if I hurt Gem," Roan drawled. "She seems to bring out the protective instinct in most men. But relax, brother. She's too perfect for me to want to damage her in any way. I'll take good care of her, you can believe it."

After a moment's hesitation while Derek seemed to be weighing the sincerity of Roan's statement, he finally swung away to the door of the room. He paused with one hand on the knob and looked back at Gem supportively. "Call me if you need me, Gem . . . anytime."

"I will, Derek," Gem answered firmly, smiling at him encouragingly. "So long."

"So long, Gem . . . Roan . . ." Derek took his leave after giving his brother a hard look.

Roan merely nodded his head, and as Gem looked up at him she could see a muscle working in his jaw, as though he were laboring under some strong emotion, which she suspected was a combination of regret and anger that, because of her, he and Derek were at odds with each other.

As the door closed behind Derek, Gem took a deep breath, then moved away from Roan's arm. "I'd better get dressed," she said with a flat lack of emotion she was far from feeling.

Roan regarded her for a moment with narrowed eyes, then shrugged. "If you insist," he said softly, his gaze caressing as he looked at her still-damp body wrapped in the towel. But Gem wasn't in the mood for love at the moment, and she disregarded his veiled invitation and moved to place her suitcase on the bed so she could extract fresh clothing. As she was turning away with her things in her hand, her eyes caught the flash of the jewels in Pedro's necklace where it lay on the bedside table. Her jaw firmed as she glanced over her shoulder to see that Roan was gazing out the window of the room, and with one swift motion she caught up the necklace in her hand before moving toward the bathroom.

"Are you shy, Gem?" Roan's voice was mocking as he moved to block her way.

Startled by his words and his abrupt movement when she had thought he was otherwise preoccupied, Gem hesitated, then lifted her chin to look back at him calmly and with a hint of defiance. "Yes," she admitted truthfully. "I'm not used to dressing in front of a man."

A sardonic glint came into Roan's eyes as he lifted a hand to cup the back of her neck and rub it seductively. "You soon will be," he asserted in a low, possessive voice. "I can promise you that."

Gem swallowed, her flesh prickling with arousal at Roan's touch. "No doubt I will," she said huskily, "but it will take a little time."

Roan gave a slight shake of his head as he shifted his hand to bring it down to the edge of the towel and run his fingers just inside its protection. "Do you think so?" he queried softly, mockingly, his smile deepening as he felt Gem's quick intake of breath. "Somehow, I don't."

Gem, already longing for him to dispense with the towel and take full possession of what he now only teased, found herself agreeing with him. She swayed slightly toward him, her eyes displaying an invitation, but to her disappointment Roan drew back, and his eyes grew hooded and unrevealing as he abruptly changed the subject.

"Who is Pedro?" he asked with soft menace.

Gem stepped back, blinking up at him in surprise as he caught her off guard.

"You named your truck after him, you wear his necklace . . ." Roan continued, his tone hard. "What does he mean to you?"

Gem shook her head in puzzlement at the jealous note in Roan's voice. "He's . . . he's my oldest friend," she stammered out, her eyes wide. "We grew up together. He's like a brother to me."

Roan continued to regard her with muted suspicion for a long moment before he relaxed slightly. "I'd rather you didn't see him unless I'm with you," he finally said, though his tone had softened somewhat.

"But, Roan . . ." Gem started to protest, then let the words die in her throat as it dawned on her that Roan's jealousy was a positive sign. Quickly she dropped her eyes as she instinctively realized it would be better not to let him see her thoughts. She almost told him that it was unlikely she would see Pedro anyway since he lived so far away, but on second thought she decided to keep that to herself. Instead she said, "I don't know if he would want to see me after I start living with you, anyway. He's one of those silly romantics who believe in love and marriage." She thought it wise to conceal the fact that Pedro was himself engaged, and she almost giggled when Roan bristled again.

"I'll be damned if you're going to spend time with other men while you're living with me! When you come into my house, you're mine!"

Gem faced him, thoroughly pleased by his possessiveness, though she wondered if he realized *why* he felt so possessive toward her. "How about my father?" she asked with a straight face, her tone containing only very mild, very sweet mockery. "If he decides not to kill you, I *had* planned to visit him from time to time."

Roan's reaction was an amused chuckle. "Jim may *want* to kill me, I'll grant you that. But he won't. And when you do see him, I'd prefer you didn't stay overnight."

Gem bristled at that! "Now wait a minute!" she challenged him. "I may be coming to live with you, but you won't own me! If I want to go and stay with my parents occasionally, I'll do so, whether you like it or not!"

Her rebellion was short-lived as Roan moved closer to her and took her into his arms. He kissed her, long and thoroughly enough that she was soon compliant in his arms. When he raised his head to gaze with sensuous amusement into her softened eyes, he shook his head slightly as he slowly began to unwrap her from her towel. "I don't think the subject will come up too often, honey," he said with soft meaning. "I think you're going to like my bed so much, you're not going to want to spend your nights anywhere else."

And as Gem melted to his touch upon her already fevered body, she was almost entirely certain that he was quite right. What she was not so certain of, though she fervently hoped time would prove her wrong, was whether Roan would come to regard her presence in his bed a necessity as well . . . for the rest of their lives.

CHAPTER ELEVEN

A sharp, unladylike expletive left Gem's lips as she struggled to tie the shimmering metallic sash at her waist and snagged the delicate fabric with a nick in one long tapering fingernail. Then Roan was behind her with his powerful hands at her waist, turning her to face him.

"Hush," he murmured, his dark eyes assessing her flushed, mutinous features reflectively. "I'll do it. If I'd known how nervous you were going to get over a simple social function, I wouldn't have insisted we go."

Gem's stormy gray eyes flashed resentment at him. "It's not a simple social function, and you know it," she said sulkily. "My parents will be there!" She started to say more, then closed her mouth against the arguments that had already failed to move him before they had accepted the invitation.

"Hmmm . . ." Roan raised one dark eyebrow as he finished tying her sash and ran his eyes over her, their expression unreadable. "If you were so worried about their being embarrassed at your appearing with me in public, I wonder why you found it necessary to wear something quite so . . ." His glance at Gem's barely covered bosom finished the statement for him. The top she wore had thin spaghetti straps tapering down to a clinging material that barely covered her breasts, left her back almost entirely bare, and extended to hip level over her narrow black skirt. The sash Roan had tied cinched in her slender waist, and the green and silver stripes of the top glimmered at every movement. It was a sophisticated, provocative, very sexy outfit, and one which was definitely not Gem's normal style.

Her bottom lip thrust out at his comment, making her look like a naughty though sexually precocious child. "I decided I might as well play my role to the hilt," she rasped at him, her eyes holding his steadily, though it was hard when she saw the disapproval gathering there. "Besides," she added with unamused teasing, "there's nothing wrong with this outfit. You'll see other women there with as little or less on."

"You're not other women," Roan rasped back in his turn. "You're not . . ." Whatever he'd been about to say he bit back, and his eyes had an unfathomable expression as he stepped away from her, giving a casual shrug of his powerful shoulders. "Wear what you like," he said, dismissing the issue uncaringly. "If there's any chastising to be done, I'll let your father do it."

His mocking intonation raked Gem's already sensitized nerves, but apart from biting back a retort she gave no sign that Roan had scored a hit with his comment. His mockery stemmed from the fact that he had never, not once in the two months they had lived together, shown the slightest inclination to back away from the disapproval of anyone who cared for Gem regarding their living arrangements . . . not her father and certainly not her mother; not even Derek could dent his determination to live his life exactly as he pleased. It was Gem who suffered silently from the pity and the anger and the sadness of her loved ones, even as she became more and more enmeshed in her love for Roan with each day she lived in his home.

Turning back to the mirror to finish applying her makeup with shaking hands, Gem reflected sadly on the hurt her behavior was inflicting on her family . . . at least on her father. Strangely enough, her mother, who had always in the past been so concerned with maintaining social standing, had shown a remarkable degree of understanding at Gem's dilemma. While she didn't approve, it had taken only one meeting with Roan for her to understand why Gem was suddenly behaving so uncharacteristically. Gem knew she would never get such understanding from her father, though she had his forgiveness.

Outraged at first, Jim Reasoner, after a long talk with Gem that left him frustrated and angry and, less to his liking, helpless, had accepted her decision without withdrawing his love. But Gem was under no illusions as to his true feelings. He was hurt and angry to the core on behalf of his treasured daughter and would never understand Roan's failure to appreciate what he held so lightly, yet so possessively.

For Roan was possessive. Gem had despaired of understanding that trait in the man she had come to love so deeply and had given her complete loyalty to, but it was at least some emotional solace. She could take hope that his determined ownership meant he might come to love her in return, though she was beginning to wonder how much longer she could wait for that to happen. Living on hope was proving to be very wearing no matter how much she loved Roan.

"Are you almost ready?" Roan stood watching her in the mirror, his stance easy and totally male. And even her dread of the coming evening didn't prevent Gem from responding to the sheer magnetism he exuded.

"Yes," she said with a deep sigh, though she wasn't. However, she was accustomed by now to adopting a facade that covered her inner ambiguity over her situation. Her head was always held high, her look direct, her husky tones never giving an inch to anyone who dared seem judgmental. She knew she had Roan's respect for maintaining that facade, if not for the fact that she considered any facade necessary. His nature made him unsympathetic toward convention, and he had expressed his irritation at what he viewed as Gem's cowardice more than once. She had given up trying to make him understand that her feelings had nothing to do with conventionality. It was her very principles and character that were affronted at the waste she perceived in their relationship. Where there could have been mutual love and loyalty and commitment, there was only a physical attraction on his part covering a void within that she wanted so much to fill with love.

Now he came to place his warm, powerful hands on her shoulders, the heat of his body touching the length of hers and, as always, melting her against him. "We won't stay long," he husked against the smooth skin of her neck. "That dress has me wishing we weren't going at all, and I have the feeling I won't be able to resist it indefinitely."

Gem closed her eyes against her inevitable arousal. "Whatever you wish," she said in her low, throaty voice, feeling her submission tauten his body as it always did. He accepted her occasional differences of opinion with him with patience and respect and tolerance, qualities she had been delighted to find in him. But in their physical relationship he was content with nothing less than total abdication of her will to his.

Later, at the party, Gem was surprised and grateful to find it turning out to be much less of a strain than she had anticipated. Apart from the veiled sadness in her father's gray eyes when he had greeted her and Roan, there had been no hint of condemnation of her chosen life-style in the demeanor of anyone she saw. She wondered rather cynically if people accepted her behavior so easily because she was a songwriter, and now that two of her songs were climbing the charts, she was becoming a *successful* songwriter. Was artists' behavior perhaps judged by different standards than ordinary people's? If so, she found the principle hypocritical, regardless of the boon such an attitude was proving to be to her nerves.

Roan's eyes were on her often throughout the evening, a habit she had at first found disconcerting but which she now enjoyed as it affirmed his continued interest. Now, as she looked up to find their brown liquidity stroking her visually, she smiled at Roan, then began to frown as she saw his eyes suddenly grow cool as he stared at something behind and to the left of her. Then she felt a slight touch on her bare shoulder accompanied by an attractive male voice inquiring, "Miss Reasoner?"

Gem swung around to find herself facing a well known, very

attractive, and at the moment, very malely appreciative country and western singing star who was one of her own particular favorites. She gaped at him like a teenager, her gray eyes widening with pleasure and star-struck awe. "Billy Martin?" she faltered increduously. "Is it really you?"

He laughed, his blue eyes crinkling at the corners attractively, his white smile devastatingly charming. Then, affecting the same manner Gem had displayed at seeing who *he* was, he said, "Gem Reasoner? The songwriter? Is it really you?"

Gem stared at him in confusion, then blushed, then echoed his laughter. "The very same," she answered pertly. "Though I wouldn't have thought someone as famous as you would recognize *my* name."

He adopted a guise of wide-eyed innocence. "Are you kidding? How do you think I got to be famous? Any singer worth his salt keeps his eyes out for good songwriters." And then with a teasing look he added, "Which is why I've been stalking you for half the night. I want to talk to you, young lady. I hope you've got some more songs stashed away that aren't already committed to . . ."

Roan's deep, challenging tones interrupted Billy incisively. "Here you are, Gem." And then with a measuring glance at Billy Martin that made that young man's smile falter slightly, he asked, "Are you going to introduce us?" His dark eyes swung to Gem, and she hid a smile at recognizing the jealousy in their expression.

"Surely Billy Martin doesn't need any introduction," she said levelly, holding Roan's eyes without a quaver. "Roan Christianson . . . Billy Martin." She made herself relax as she saw the two men shake hands while their eyes clashed. Billy's were the first to drop as he turned to Gem again, and she almost grinned as she saw their rueful acknowledgment that he had met his match. She would have been willing to bet that hadn't happened often in his life, especially since he had obtained fame and fortune.

A second later Billy went on to show he understood that Roan in some way needed to be deferred to where she was concerned.

"Would you mind, Mr. Christianson, if Miss Reasoner and I talked shop for a while? I have a feeling we'd make a good team in the music world."

Gem was certain Billy Martin's words had been entirely innocent of any ulterior meaning, but she tensed as she saw the unmistakable signs that Roan was not so sure. "*We'd* be pleased to listen," Roan said with hard smoothness, the pronoun making it clear that he had no intention of allowing Gem to accompany the other man anywhere alone.

After a momentary hesitation Billy Martin nodded. "Fine. Shall we get a drink and go out on the patio? It's a little noisy in here to talk."

Roan gave a curt nod, ignoring Gem's glare as he took her elbow and started steering her toward the nearest waiter. He released her as he swooped two glasses of champagne from the waiter's tray, but after handing her one he took possession of her arm again and walked between her and Billy as they made their way to the patio.

Despite her resentment at Roan's interference in *her* career, five minutes later she was gaping at him in astonishment as he conducted a fast-paced, knowledgeable negotiation with Billy Martin that soon had everything spelled out in crystal clear form, with nothing left to do but put the terms in writing. Since he had succeeded in winning her far more than she could have herself, she had little reason to feel resentment toward him, but she did! He had not once even bothered to ask if she *wanted* to make an arrangement with Billy to sing her songs. She did, but she considered that beside the point at the moment.

"Now just a minute!" she sputtered angrily even as the two men were shaking hands to seal their bargain. "Would either of you be the slightest bit interested in how *I* feel about all this?" Her tone dripped with sarcasm, making Billy swing around to look at her in surprise, while Roan merely cocked an ironic eyebrow at her.

"Certainly, Gem," he drawled smoothly. "Perhaps we have

been a little precipitate. I take it you're not interested in writing for Billy?"

At Billy's look of chagrin Gem felt exasperated and a little ashamed, but Roan's silky tone hadn't fooled her one bit. "You know darned well I am!" she retorted heatedly.

Roan shrugged, the golden lights in his eyes dancing with amusement as he raised both eyebrows at her with innocent question. "Then you didn't like the terms we agreed on," he stated, as though that must be the cause of her irritation.

Gem fumed. "You know they were perfectly all right!" she snarled at him, refraining from admitting they were far more generous than she would have expected or asked for. As Roan continued to wait with exaggerated patience for her to spell out why she was behaving so outrageously, she took a deep breath and said with deadly sweetness, "It's just that I prefer to be consulted when deals are made in my name, Roan, *darling.*" Her endearment was nothing close to affectionate, and Roan's sardonic smile acknowledged the fact. But when he said nothing more, Gem was left floundering, and she glared at him even more stonily. "In the future please remember that!" she pronounced with more bravado than she felt, and then she turned on her heel and left the two of them standing there staring at her retreating back. It was, perhaps, just as well that she didn't hear their exchange following her departure.

Billy looked at Roan after tearing admiring eyes away from Gem's deliciously smooth back. "Is she yours?" he asked with a careful lack of emphasis in his tone.

"Completely." Roan's voice and eyes left no doubt that he was fully capable of holding what he claimed—and fully prepared to do so.

Billy gave a resigned sigh, a defeated shrug, and then a charming grin as he sliced his eyes back to Roan. "Enough said," he conceded gracefully. "I never compete when defeat is certain. However"—and his tone grew a little wistful and his eyes were speculative as he eyed Roan consideringly—"if you're ever stupid enough to lose her, I feel it's only fair to warn you I'll be waiting in the wings. I'm a very patient man when there's something worth waiting for, and she"—he nodded his head in the direction Gem had taken—"she's one in a million. Better marry her if you plan on keeping her. She's that kind of woman, and there'll be plenty of others willing if you're not . . . including me."

Without waiting for Roan to reply Billy Martin strode away, his straight back and charming grin concealing the hint of chances lost in his clear blue eyes. Roan watched him go, his jaw tensed, his brown eyes thoughtful and considering and more than a little angry. And then with an impatient movement of his broad shoulders he went to find Gem and take her to the one place where he was free from his nagging, irritating need for her because there she was completely his.

Some little while later, as they entered their bedroom in the house Gem was slowly managing to turn into a home rather than merely a residence, Roan eyed Gem's still stiff, ramrod-straight shoulders, and a little smile played over his beautifully formed, sensuous mouth. He moved with lazy grace to his bureau and extracted a package from the interior of one of the drawers, and his smile turned to a charming grin when he faced her and saw she was eyeing him curiously though warily.

"I bought you something," he said with unaccustomed self-deprecating mockery. "I've been looking for it ever since . . ." He hesitated, then said, "Well, for quite some time. Here." He held it out to her, and when she didn't immediately take it, he raised one of her hands and placed it there. Then he turned away and started pulling off his tie, whistling a tuneless melody that was curiously pleasant to Gem's ears despite his lack of music sense.

Hesitantly Gem opened the box he had handed her, then froze when she saw what was there. Duplicates of the earrings he had given her at their first meeting nestled in the box, along with a matching necklace which put Pedro's to shame. Tears moistened Gem's eyes as she wished with all her heart that Roan's gift had the same meaning Pedro's had . . . that it had been given with love rather than out of a desire to place his brand on her body. Or better yet, she thought with aching sadness, she would have preferred a plain, solid-gold wedding band to these meaningless diamonds and emeralds, whose only value was monetary.

She felt Roan behind her and blinked her tears away stoically. "Do you like them?" he asked low-voiced, and if she had let her imagination run away with her, she would have fancied she heard a hint of anxiety in his tone. But she had begun to learn to put fantasy where Roan was concerned away from her out of pure self-protection.

"Thank you, Roan," she said tonelessly. "They're . . . lovely."

She felt his momentary stillness, then heard his displeasure at her reaction in his harshness. "Give them to me. I want to put them on you."

Silently Gem handed the box to Roan, keeping her eyes down as he extracted the baubles from the box and fastened the necklace around her neck. He hesitated with the earrings in his hand, then shrugged. "I suppose bed is not the place for earrings," he said wryly. "You can wear them another time."

Gem nodded, still not speaking, and then felt Roan's hand lifting her chin. She kept her face expressionless as Roan studied her, though she knew by his tight-lipped frown that he saw the moistness on her lashes. "Are you crying from gratitude or because you're disappointed?" he asked dryly.

Gem stared into his eyes blankly. "I'm not crying," she said softly, using every ounce of her will to keep her voice steady.

It was almost her undoing when something unknowable flashed behind Roan's dark eyes for an instant before he leaned his head down to kiss the moisture away from her long black lashes. An aching yearning tore at her breast as she longed for that tender action to be more than what it signified, yet knew it couldn't be.

"Come to bed," Roan whispered, lifting her into his arms and carrying her there. "If you won't speak what you feel, you can show me."

And Gem did, with every fiber of her love in every touch,

every kiss, every soft cry of his name, and every shudder where his hands brought her to his will. She failed to note that Roan was shaken, perhaps for the first time since she'd known him, by the quality of her giving because she didn't expect such a reaction from him. Nor did he. And long after Gem lay sleeping in exhaustion, curled against his body like a tired child, he lay staring up at the dark ceiling, glaring at it with a grimness that, had it been animate, would have given it pause for concern.

CHAPTER TWELVE

Gem awoke to find a note on the pillow beside her, informing her that Roan would be gone for several days on business. She sighed, missing him, yet at the same time relieved that she would have a few days to lock him out of her heart and mind and soul while she worked on a new song that had been boiling in her head for days. She needed the peace his absences provided, though in truth they had been few and far between since she had come to live with him. This had puzzled her, as she had understood that Roan traveled extensively in his business, but she had shrugged it away, thinking he had merely hit a slow season.

As she climbed from bed to take a shower and begin her day, she would have been astounded if she could have known that Roan had forced himself away from her side as an exercise in self-discipline, and that his temper, as volatile as ever, almost cost him two leases before the trip was over, cut short by two days by his unwelcome, almost savage desire to get back to her.

Gem had just finished putting the final touches to her new song when Roan arrived back unexpectedly one evening, his expression thunderous, his eyes anything but glad to see her though they were hungry in their assessment when she stood before him barefooted, blue-jeaned, and in an old plaid shirt, with her hair tied back in a ponytail.

"Roan?" she faltered warily, struggling for cheerfulness but perturbed by the contradictory emotions she saw flickering in his eyes. "I didn't expect you back this soon."

"Sorry if I upset any of your plans," Roan said dryly, his eyes narrowing suspiciously.

"No," Gem hastened to reassure him. "I just finished a song. I haven't been out of the house since you left."

Roan's jaw tightened, though the look in his eyes softened. "No? Well, then it's time you did get out," he said more reasonably. "I need some relaxation myself. I thought we'd run over to a cabin I own near Lake Texhoma. Do some fishing. Are you interested?"

Slowly Gem began to relax. Her imagination must have been playing tricks on her, she thought. She nodded eagerly. "It sounds great! I love to fish!" She moved closer to him, smiling, taking a loving assessment of her own. "You do look tired," she said softly. "When do you want to go?"

"Tonight," Roan answered, reaching for her, pulling her close to his body with a careful lack of need in his touch, though his eyes closed to shut away the expression in them from observation. Gem molded herself to him eagerly, less skilled than he at hiding her need to feel him against her. After a long moment of holding each other Roan drew back, his eyes hooded as he gazed down at her. "Don't I get a kiss hello?" he murmured sensuously. "Or didn't you miss me?"

Gem's gray eyes were luminous as she raised them to his. "I always miss you when you're gone," she confessed helplessly, parting her lips with a soft sigh of satisfaction as Roan's moved closer. The restraint both exercised in the kiss spelled out their need more clearly than any greed might have done. When Roan drew back, however, the brown in his eyes had deepened to velvet, and he whispered, "Come upstairs. We can wait a little while before we start."

Gem was nodding her assent even as she tucked her head into the hollow of his shoulder as he turned her toward the stairs. With her eyes down she missed the gleam of satisfied male possession, coupled with almost savage resentment that shone from Roan's.

But once they were locked into the privacy of their bedroom, his ambiguous feelings were expressed physically, in the roughness of his possession of her as well as the periods of magic tenderness that drew sobs of welcome from Gem. She responded to both equally fervently, holding nothing back from him, as was ever the case in the only place where she could express her love without revealing it in words.

"God, I needed you," Roan said with a shudder when it was over, surprising Gem with the depths of feeling in his tone. Before she had time to react to his revelation, however, he withdrew from her, averting his head so that she couldn't see his expression. He headed for the bathroom, his tone carefully neutral as he instructed her to get packed. "Don't take anything fancy," he said unnecessarily, as though she would be so foolish as to pack an evening gown for a fishing trip. "In fact"—his smile was mockingly rakish as he finally turned his head in her direction—"you don't need to take very much at all. I don't intend to spend all my time fishing."

Gem couldn't suppress a shiver of anticipation at his unspoken promise, and it was with a brilliant smile and eager movements that she sprang from the bed to begin pulling a pair of her oldest jeans from a drawer. She was unashamedly, spontaneously singing when she entered the bathroom to pack her toiletries for the trip, even going so far as to wink mischievously at Roan as he passed her on his way out. His grin was natural and unstrained, completely captivating as he swatted her bottom before continuing on into the bedroom to do his own packing.

Gem grinned to herself as she thought about the lavender teddy she had packed as a special treat for Roan . . . not that she was under any illusions that she would be allowed to keep it on for any length of time, but it would be fun to see his reaction to it.

Roan proved to be in an exceptionally good mood on their drive to the lake, and Gem thoroughly enjoyed the trip. She reveled in his teasing humor, and her eyes sparkled with interest as he opened up to her more than he ever had before about his thoughts and feelings in many areas, though not about what he felt for her. But then she didn't expect any startling, sudden declaration of love, which was all she really wanted to hear in that area.

The cabin on the lake was delightfully compact, and after putting away the groceries they had bought on the way, the two of them went for a walk on the lakeshore. It was too late to fish, and they were tired from the drive, but they were in a perfect mood to enjoy the shimmer of the moon on the water and the quiet and peace of the area.

Gem treasured the easy relaxation that Roan displayed, softening his rugged features almost into gentleness. She delighted in the strong, encompassing support of his arm around her waist as they walked, and the hint of tenderness in his voice when he spoke to her. "It's good to be here with you," he said once with spontaneous naturalness, and she smiled her own happiness back at him.

He kissed her just before they started back, and it was a long, slow kiss, filled with sweet promises, and it ended only with his arousal and growing sense of urgency to get back to the cabin and make love to her. "Come on," he murmured huskily. "If we can't fish, there are other pleasures to be had."

Back in the cabin Gem resisted Roan's attempt to draw her to bed. "Not yet," she whispered mischievously. "I have something I want to show you first."

Dark eyebrows rose in amused question, but Roan let her go to her suitcase, where she rustled inside it, then hid what she withdrew from his sight as she hastened to the tiny bathroom. When she came out, her slender body encased in the sheer, voluptuously clinging lavender teddy, the lights in the outer room were extinguished, and Roan lay in bed watching her where she stood outlined against the light of the bathroom behind her.

She heard the catch in his breath from across the room, her skin prickling at this evidence that he found her pleasing. "Do you like it?" she crooned throatily.

He teased her huskily. "I'm not sure. You'll have to come closer so I can get a better look."

Gem pouted. "You can't see in the dark," she protested sulkily.

"Trust me. I have eyes like a cat." Roan chuckled. "But you can leave the bathroom light on if you like. I don't mind having a little extra illumination."

Gem exaggerated her walk as she crossed to him, playing the vamp with childish glee, and then pouncing on Roan in mock anger when he laughed at her attempted seductiveness. "Hey!" he protested laughingly as she pummeled him with her fists. "If you're going to seduce me, this is no way to go about it! You're supposed to stroke me, not attack me!"

"You don't deserve seduction," Gem growled at him threateningly. "In fact, I think I'll . . ." She got no further with her threat to leave him, as he neatly flipped her onto her back and covered her body with his own, pinning her arms above her head in a grip she struggled against futilely.

"Maybe I don't," he admitted with a low chuckle. "But in that outfit *you* certainly do. Would you like me to show you how a serious seducer goes about it?"

"You already have!" Gem said grumpily. "More than once, in fact!" But her mock glare faded as she saw the gleam of intent in Roan's eyes deepen. "Of course," she said, her tone speculative, "if you think you have anything *new* to show me . . ." Her tone expressed her doubts that he had.

"Oh, honey," he crooned mockingly, taking up her challenge, "you're going to be sorry you said that . . . or maybe you won't be," he added, the totally male consideration with which he was regarding her causing chills to chase up and down her spine. "On second thought maybe you're ready for the next step in your education. There's a lot I haven't taught you yet."

"There couldn't be," Gem regarded him doubtfully, half-afraid, half-eager to see if he spoke the truth.

"Don't count on it, darlin'," he said, his tone dropping another notch until it was a seductive growl. "I've been holding back until I thought you were ready to grow up a little more. Are you ready now, baby?"

Gem wasn't sure what she was letting herself in for, but there was no resisting the promise in Roan's tone. Her breathing quickening, she slowly nodded her assent, then relaxed into her senses as Roan began to show her what he meant.

She relaxed even further as he started out in much the same way he always did when he had the patience to resist the urges that often dominated him as well as her. A sleepy, sensuous smile curved her mouth as he feathered her cheeks, her throat, her shoulders with light, erotic kisses. She sucked in her breath when his hand came up to her breast, lifting it still encased in the lavender sheerness so that most of it spilled from the material, then nuzzling the fullness he held with tantalizing lightness.

"Roan . . ." She breathed his name from deep in her throat and felt his smile against her skin. Then he was gone from there and traveling downward, his mouth blazing through the soft material she wore as though it didn't exist. Lower he went, until Gem's eyes were open and staring, her breathing becoming more rapid, the tremors Roan's mouth evoked rippling over her flesh.

"Roan?" The question in her voice came out in a gasp, and then a groan, as she felt him unsnap the fastening of the teddy between her limp thighs.

"Hush, baby," he whispered smilingly as the last snap came undone and he pushed the material aside and replaced it with questing fingers. "Just relax and enjoy. This is your turn."

Her foggy brain didn't take in the implications of his last statement. She was too immersed in doing exactly as he instructed and enjoying to the fullest the pleasure he gave so exquisitely. In any case she didn't have time to think as his mouth replaced his fingers and she felt the darting thrust of his tongue exploding against her flesh as though a rocket had gone off inside her.

She arched against him spasmodically, crying his name. "Roan! Don't! Ah, God, I can't . . ." Ecstasy choked off her words as Roan paid no heed to them, concentrating instead on drawing out her pleasure until she went spinning into a realm of sensation so overwhelming, it swamped her mind, choked off thought, replaced it with a totally self-involved, greedy concentration on her burning need. Relentless with his provocation, Roan pushed her to the brink, but when she was about to topple over the edge, he withdrew, making her cry out her protest in an agonized sob.

Rising to his knees, Roan stripped her of her garment, then pulled her on top of him, tangling one hand in her hair as he kissed her, his mouth rough with his own need. But after a moment it became gentle and searching, making Gem ache with the potential for giving she saw in him, making her want to give back what he had so freely given her.

Not really certain how to express what she was feeling, she began to copy his delightful lovemaking, feathering his face and the strong column of his neck with kisses, then easing down to seek out his chest and male nipples with her soft lips and darting tongue. Roan lay quiescent under her tender ministrations, only a slight shudder and his rasping breath indicating his pleasure in her reciprocation; but as she eased lower his hand tightened in her hair, starting to tug downward once, then stopping to move restlessly over her scalp with caressing fingers.

Gem had picked up on that hesitant downward pressure, however, and swallowed down her slight nervousness as she interpreted his need. For Roan she would do anything . . . venture down entirely new paths . . . to express the love and the need to give she felt flooding her senses. Slowly she eased farther down, feeling him tense as he defined her destination.

"You don't have to . . ." he started to say, but his voice shook for all its strength, and it was that that made Gem melt with the desire to please him.

"I want to . . ." she murmured huskily. "Show me, Roan . . . help me . . ." And as she followed his direction she became immersed in this new experience, then awed by the power she came to have over him and by his control as he stopped himself on the same brink he had refused to let her cross earlier.

With a suddenness that made her gasp, he seized her waist and lifted her bodily above him with a strength that thrilled and astonished her, then settled her upon him in a position he had never shown her before and which she found awakened a need in her to have the upper hand for once in their lovemaking. Not that she really did—only the semblance of it—but it was enough to throw her into a fury of mock domination, so that their mating took on a power that brought sounds from Roan she had never heard him make before.

The culmination of their lovemaking was no more than a degree above the satisfaction they had already reached together by the time it came. And when it was done, Roan surprised her again by enfolding her fiercely in his arms to hold her against him in a grip that threatened to stop her already scarce breath, as he rocked her and murmured incoherent mumblings that pleased and enchanted her with their spontaneity.

At last they lay quietly together until Gem stretched languorously and gave in to the mischievous urge to tease Roan. "Well," she said in a speculative tone, "it seems I wasn't as close to graduation as I thought. Do you suppose I'm anywhere near to getting my cap and gown now?"

Roan gave an exhausted chuckle, pulling her against him with a rough jerk. "God, woman, am I creating an insatiable monster here?" he growled. "Don't you think you've learned enough for one night?"

Gem considered that for a moment in silence. Then finally she announced in a positive tone, "Uh-uh. I want to get my doctorate."

Roan laughed helplessly as he turned to face her, cuddling her pliant form against him with gentle hands. "Okay," he said in an exaggeratedly tired voice. "Just be gentle with me, hmmm? I'm older than you are, and my energy tends to run down about dawn."

Gem stroked him with loving tenderness. "Really?" she asked with innocent interest. "Since when? I seem to recall . . ."

"*Shut up!*" Roan murmured distinctly, and then enforced her compliance by taking her mouth in a kiss that gave very little indication his strength and energy were nearly as depleted as he had claimed.

By the time their long weekend was over, they had very few fish to show for it, but if their tired, contented smiles were any indication, they had found something else more valuable, and in Gem's case, at least, she felt she had gone far beyond a mere doctorate and on into the realm of sheer genius in the art of love.

CHAPTER THIRTEEN

Whatever secret hopes Gem might have started cherishing in her deepest subconscious that there might be some chance for her and Roan to develop a more permanent relationship as a result of their idyllic weekend were dashed to oblivion shortly after their return.

True, Roan seemed more relaxed and easy than she had ever seen him, but his increased confidence in her merely seemed to reassure him that whatever they shared could have no lasting hold on him. His urgent possessiveness of her diminished, causing a chill to settle in the region of her heart as he actually encouraged her to meet with Billy Martin alone regarding her new song. Then Roan left again, a bare two days after they returned from the lake, with the stated intention of being gone for a couple of weeks.

Gem faced her fears that this was the beginning of the end, feeling empty and hollow inside, all the more so since the weekend had promised so much. But she had taken Roan's warnings not to count on him more to heart than she had realized, it seemed, and her inner resources allowed her to function, if not to find joy in the functioning.

Billy Martin did his best to ease the depression fighting to take hold of her, his charm overriding her objections when he insisted he take her out to dinner the night before they were to get together for a working session on the song.

"Billy, really," she protested when he called her to make the date, "I'm . . . not . . . er, feeling very well. I wouldn't be good company."

"All the more reason you should get out and enjoy yourself," he retorted irrepressibly. "I carry a surefire remedy around with me for the doldrums."

"Oh, yes?" Gem asked dryly. "Do you sing them away?"

A sly chuckle greeted her ears. "Are you trying to pry my secret out of me?" He made a chiding sound over the phone. "That's underhanded and sneaky, lady, and furthermore it won't work. If you want a demonstration, you're going to have to have dinner with me to get it."

Gem smiled a little forlornly, looking around her at the huge, empty confines of her self-imposed prison. Suddenly she was fed up with ambling around inside Roan's huge house like a solitary ghost, and she was even more fed up with anticipating the worst and letting that anticipation dominate her emotions. If she was going to survive without Roan, it was time she began the process before the loss was actually forced upon her.

"All right, Billy," she said, her tone lightening with her mood, "you talked me into it. But you'd better have that remedy ready, or you'll be the one who suffers. Are you sure you want to risk it?"

Billy's pleased chuckle came over the wire, reassuring her that he did, indeed, want to risk it. "It's working already," he said with smug self-satisfaction, "and this is just over the phone. Wait till I apply it in person!"

With a laugh at the realization that Billy was entirely correct —she did feel better just from talking to him—Gem took him to task for his conceit, then rang off after he had instructed her to dress western. Since Gem didn't feel in the least like dressing up anyway, she was more than happy to comply.

That evening, as Gem stood in front of the downstairs hall mirror putting on a pale gray Stetson that set off her black hair and gray eyes to perfection, she grinned at herself and stuck out her tongue. She was ready to be distracted from her brooding thoughts, and as the doorbell announced Billy's arrival she intercepted the servant who had come to answer it and threw open the door herself to greet Billy.

He stood leaning against the doorframe with a long, thin cheroot hanging from his mouth, his western hat tipped low over his eyes, his thumbs linked in the belt loops of his faded jeans, which were held up by a leather belt sporting a huge brass buckle with *Billy* emblazoned across it, and one booted foot crossed over the other.

"Howdy, ma'am," he said in a slow, laconic Texas drawl. "I heard tell there was a lady bein' held prisoner in this here dungeon. You know anythin' about it?"

Gem immediately fell into his game. She pressed both hands to her cheeks, her huge eyes wide and frightened over them. "Yes," she whispered with a furtive look over her shoulder. "Black Bart has her chained up in the attic! But he's a mean one, mister. Are you sure you can handle him?"

Slowly Billy pulled himself up to his full height, threw back his shoulders, and hitched his jeans up in a macho gesture. "Lady, I can handle anythin'," he drawled with disgusting assurance. "Just lead me to him!"

Gem looked doubtfully at his hips. "But you don't even have a six-shooter!" she wailed in reproach. "And Black Bart has a shotgun! You can't go in there bare-handed!"

Billy hesitated, took the cheroot from his lips, and flicked ashes with a thoughtful frown on his face. Then he peered up at her from beneath glowering brows. "Hmmm . . . a shotgun, did you say?"

Gem nodded vigorously, her eyes widening even further in innocent agreement. Then with a sly, sheepish grin on his handsome face, Billy suddenly grabbed Gem's arm, pulled her out the door with a flourish, wrapped an arm about her waist, and hustled her down the stairs toward his waiting country Cadillac . . . a spotless red pickup truck.

"But mister!" Gem wailed, looking back over her shoulder at the house as Billy pulled her along. "What about the lady in the attic?"

"To hell with *her*!" Billy shouted gleefully as he pulled open the passenger door of the pickup and thrust Gem inside. "Bart can have her! You don't think I'm going to face his shotgun when I've already got you, do you?"

He slammed the door then and hustled around the front of the pickup to climb inside in haste, then gunned the motor and screeched out the driveway on two wheels, as if being pursued by a posse.

"Sir, I feel it my duty to inform you that you're nothing but a dirty, low-down, yellow-bellied coward!" Gem asserted primly as she hung on for dear life when Billy swung around a corner on two wheels.

"Right!" Billy agreed with a gleeful laugh. "And I plan to stay that way for a longggg time!"

Gem dissolved into laughter then, admonishing Billy to slow down between gasps. "You won't live long if you keep up this speed!" she chortled. "And more to the point, neither will I!"

Immediately Billy took his foot off the accelerator, placed both hands on the wheel in a perfect ten-two position, and began to drive with all the caution of an eighty-year-old man, looking fearfully around at the other cars on the street as though he expected one of them to ram into him at any moment.

"All right, all right!" Gem gave in when they had slowed to a bare five miles an hour and cars behind them were blasting them with their horns. "You can at least go the speed limit!"

Billy complied with alacrity, shooting her a broad grin as he did so. "Whatever my lady wants my lady will get tonight," he asserted with chivalrous gallantry. "I am at her service."

"Well, it's about time you remembered what a gentleman is supposed to behave like," she scolded disapprovingly. "Any man who's a little afraid of a mere shotgun . . ." She shrugged and pouted in disgust.

"Don't hold it against me, honey," he punned with a sly grin.

From then on the entire evening was upbeat and fun, and more important, Gem didn't have a spare moment to worry about Roan Christianson's love . . . or lack of it. Billy took her to a small out-of-the-way café and ordered her chicken-fried steak, french fries, and salad, which turned out to be mouth-watering, and since Billy was obviously well known there, entertaining as well. The waitresses flirted with him, the cook came out to compliment him on his latest hit, and the fat lady at the cash register bawled him out because he hadn't been in to see her for too long.

"Sorry, Mamma," he apologized teasingly, then shot his eyes to Gem and wiggled his brows suggestively. "But can you blame me?"

The fat woman subjected Gem to a thorough inspection, then pronounced judgment positively. "No, can't say as I do. Looks like you're finally gettin' some sense in that head of yours, Billy. This one looks like she might have a brain as well as a body."

Gem choked on her iced tea at that but managed to keep a straight face as Billy's eyes laughed into hers. "Oh, she does, she does, Mamma Bates," he said soberly. "And if she didn't already have six illegitimate kids, I'd ask her to marry me in a minute."

Gem did choke at that, but fortunately Mamma Bates had more sense than to believe him. "Go along with you," she scoffed. "You're a lyin' dog. She ain't no more than a kid herself."

Billy shook his head and gave a heavy sigh. "Looks can be deceivin', Mamma," he cautioned her. "She's all of forty-three . . ." He shrugged dolefully. "I'm only twenty-seven. Do you think a marriage between a younger man and an older woman has much of a chance?"

Gem sputtered, glared at him, then decided to spike his guns. "Oh, but with your latest face-lift, Billy, you don't look a day over twenty," she cooed as she inspected his handsome face critically. Then she nodded with determination as though she'd reached a decision. "I think I can put up with you for at least a couple more years. After that"—she shrugged and shook her head—"you'll be over the hill."

Mamma Bates cackled, Billy glared, and Gem smiled sweetly.

"Just for that, woman, I'm going to let Tank Williams cut in on us on the dance floor tonight," Billy threatened.

"*Tank* Williams?" Gem asked increduously through tears of laughter.

"Right!" Billy smirked. "Three hundred pounds, twelve feet tall, and sings like a bullfrog in his partners' ears."

"God!" Gem shuddered, then she eyed him speculatively. "But can he dance?" she got down to business.

Billy lifted his shoulders and spread his hands. "Sure . . . he doesn't break more than one or two female feet a night. They tell me dancin' with him is a real adventure." He reached over and patted her shoulder consolingly. "Don't worry. There's an all-night medical clinic just up the street . . . specializes in casts."

Unperturbed, Gem batted her eyes at him flirtatiously. "And would you autograph a cast for me, Mr. Martin?" she asked coyly.

"Twice," he promised solemnly. "Once on each foot."

They departed the restaurant amongst a chorus of hearty *Ya'll come back, now*'s and Billy drove them to a well known country and western club that was packed to the rafters.

Billy was a favorite here, too, it seemed, and from the moment they entered the place, they were swamped with his adoring friends and fans. Gem danced with so many good-hearted strangers, she began to get dizzy from all the spinning they seemed addicted to. Then, of course, Billy was prevailed upon to sing, and to Gem's embarrassment he insisted she come on stage with him and do a duet.

"You don't even know if I *can* sing," she whispered furiously to him, but he just grinned.

"That's what you think," he said with a superior smirk. "I have my sources." Which left Gem wondering just how far Billy had gone to find out about her, and why he would want to.

The two of them sang one of her creations, which was climbing the charts, and their voices proved surprisingly compatible. So much so, in fact, that when they finished the slow, sweet ballad, there was a moment of silence from the audience before they erupted into cheers and clapping and whistling for more.

Gem consented to just one more song, and when it was over, she determinedly resisted the audience's urging for more, as did Billy. She barely managed to stop him from announcing her as the author of the songs, however, and was relieved when, after a glance at her flushed, forbidding face, he dropped the matter.

"Shy, huh?" he teased her when they came down from the stage.

"I like my anonymity," Gem declared firmly. "And if I'd had any idea you were going to drag me up on that stage beforehand . . ." She glowered at his unrepentant grin.

"You'd have come out with me anyway, right?" he asked irrepressibly.

Toward the last of the evening, as Gem was just going to suggest they head for home, she surprised an unholy grin on Billy's face as he looked beyond her shoulder. "Ah . . ." he gave a sigh of relief. "I was afraid Tank wasn't going to make it before you were ready to go home."

"Tank!" Gem said in alarm. "You mean there really is a Tank?"

"Take a look," Billy murmured, and she heard his muffled chortle as she swung around with her eyes cast upward, expecting to see a huge hulk approaching her, and then had to lower them to the skinniest, shortest man she'd ever seen in her life.

"Tank!" Billy greeted the little man heartily. "How are you, you old son of a gun? I wondered where you'd got to tonight."

"I had to take my mother to the library," Tank answered almost absently, his eyes fixed adoringly on Gem. "Would you like to dance, miss?" he asked almost in the same breath.

"Why . . . er . . . sure," Gem agreed faintly, casting Billy a scorching look out of the corner of her eye, and then she was swept into an astonishingly strong grip as Tank pulled her into his arms.

If it hadn't been for her sense of humor, Gem would have killed Billy Martin for what he had set her up for. Tank's head came just to her breast, and he had a tenacious tendency to rest it there while they danced. Gem determinedly pulled back, and Tank, just as determinedly, clutched her closer. Over his head Gem glared at where Billy sat, his shoulders shaking with merriment, his hands covering his face to hide his laughter from Tank's eyes. Which was ridiculous, as Tank had eyes for nothing but Gem's bosom! To make things worse, Tank fancied himself a singer, and the whole time they danced, he sang along with the band in a high, quavering voice that sent ragged chills down Gem's sensitive back.

She almost gasped with relief when the song came to an end, only to have to fight off Tank's attempt to keep her out on the floor for the next song. "No, no, thank you, Tank," she told the little man firmly as she half-dragged him off the floor. "I have a headache, and Billy's going to take me home now. *Aren't* you, Billy?" she snarled at her now innocently solemn escort.

"Yes, ma'am," he answered meekly, holding out her leather fringed jacket for her to slip her arms into. "She's tired, Tank," he said apologetically to the downcast little man. "You should have got here earlier."

"I had to take my . . ." Tank started to explain again about his mother, but Billy cut him off.

"Yeah, sure, Tank. Sorry about that. Maybe next time, huh?"

And even through her halfhearted outrage at Billy's trick Gem had to give him credit for the tactful way he spoke to Tank, protecting the man's ego.

She couldn't stay angry with Billy, though she gave it a good try all the way home, and when he accompanied her up to the door, she said, "I ought to cancel our session tomorrow after what you pulled, Billy Martin. I'm not sure I want any man with such a warped sense of humor singing my precious songs." Her sniff was an indication that she was teasing, however, and Billy merely grinned down at her unapologetically.

"You're an angel for taking it like you did, honey," he said with sincere admiration. "But, then, I knew you would be."

"Hmpf!" was all Gem could find to say to such a compliment.

Then Billy surprised her completely. "Can I kiss you good night, darlin'?" he asked with boyish pleading.

Gem stepped back uncertainly. "Billy . . ."

Billy reached out a hand to tug a strand of her long, black hair. "Oh, I know you belong to Roan," he said without rancor. "But you owe me something for the medicine, don't you?"

"Medicine?" Gem asked with puzzled wariness.

"Don't you feel good now?" he asked innocently.

"Yes," Gem allowed after a second's thought, her smile rueful.

Billy lifted his shoulders in a shrug. "Then my medicine worked, didn't it?" And at Gem's laughing nod he stepped closer. "So my bill is one kiss," he said softly. "That's cheap compared to what they'd charge you at a hospital."

Gem still regarded him uncertainly, but then she shrugged. "All right, one kiss," she gave in. "I always pay my bills. But I'll want a receipt."

"Honey," Billy murmured as he took her shoulders into his strong, warm hands and slowly lowered his head to hers, "I'm an honest man. You don't really think I'd charge you more than once, do you?" But the gleam in his eyes before he closed them as his warm, soft lips enveloped hers made Gem fully aware that despite his claims otherwise Billy Martin wouldn't think twice about billing her repeatedly for the service he had rendered her that night.

His kiss was long and just demanding enough to make Gem aware that she was dealing with a very skilled lover who knew exactly how to please a woman and who was holding himself back from taking the pleasures he would like to take for himself. She responded cautiously, aware also that while Billy didn't set off the overwhelming passion inside her that Roan did, his kiss was pleasantly arousing without being unduly threatening. She was even a little disappointed when Billy at last drew back, taking small, departing sips from her lips as he did so, as though he had to break the contact gradually so as to break it at all.

The lazy satisfaction in his blue eyes revealed to Gem that he was fully aware she hadn't found his kiss unpleasant, and his drawl was self-confident when he spoke at last. "That's just a little sample I wanted to leave with you to remember in case you ever find yourself in a position to buy the whole product." And when he saw the hesitant withdrawal in Gem's clear, gray eyes, he shook his head chidingly. "Don't worry, babe. I'm not going to make a nuisance of myself. But I wanted you to know there's other fish in the sea if Roan Christianson blows his chance for paradise."

Gem's smile was warm and grateful and affectionate as Billy smiled down at her with tender sweetness. "I'll remember, Billy," she whispered.

"See that you do," he instructed her seriously. Then his humor was back as he took his leave, his step confident and insouciant. "See you at ten tomorrow morning, right?"

"Right," Gem said with soft fondness and watched as he strode whistling to his pickup, his attractive physique outlined by the gaslight on the lawn beyond the circling drive.

The house seemed to close in on Gem as she entered it, and she sighed with discouragement at its emptiness, hoping she could get to sleep without thoughts of Roan coming between her and the rest she badly needed. She had just slipped between the covers when the phone beside the bed gave a muted tinkle, and she caught up the receiver eagerly, praying it was Roan. Her heart jerked in her breast when she heard his deep tones saying her name. "Gem? It's Roan."

"Roan! Hello, dar—" She bit off the endearment, feeling constrained by her lack of security in his affections. "Hi," she covered weakly. "How are you?"

"Tired," he drawled in a tone that verified his description. "I've been trying to call you for quite a while, but you weren't home."

The faint question in his voice made her bite her lip with indecisiveness, but then she squared her shoulders and made a decision, knowing she would be almost relieved if Roan grew angry with her explanation. "I was out with Billy," she said as calmly as she could. "He took me out to dinner and then dancing."

She held her breath through the short silence that followed her statement, and then frowned in puzzlement at the disparity between Roan's strained tone and his casual words. "Good," he said without inflection. "Did you have a good time?"

She shrugged though he couldn't see her. "Yes," she said somewhat bleakly. "Billy's good company."

"I'm sure he is," was Roan's somewhat wry reply, telling Gem nothing about what he was, or wasn't, feeling. She would have been a great deal more reassured if she could have seen the scowl on his rugged features and the tautness of his jaw.

"Did . . . did you call for some special reason, Roan?" Gem asked tentatively, hoping against hope that he would say he had just wanted to hear her voice.

He didn't. Instead he said, "Yes, I wanted you to know I won't be home as soon as I thought I would. I just heard today about a place in Montana that looks promising for a lease. It will take me awhile to check it out." Gem closed her eyes against his news as he continued. "I still have a week or so here in Kansas. Then I'll head up to Montana." Her eyes came open as he asked, "What will you do while I'm gone?"

Taking a deep breath, Gem made her voice breezily unconcerned. "Oh, I'll work on some more songs as usual," she said. "Then maybe go to the ranch to see the folks for a day or two. I'm missing them"—and she was, like a little girl who needed cuddling after a big hurt—"and it's been awhile since I've been at the ranch."

"Sounds good," said Roan, and for a second Gem thought he almost sounded resentful that she was able to fill her time successfully while he was not there to fill it for her. But then his voice turned sensuous, and she forgot everything else. "I wish you were here now," he said, low-voiced. "I never noticed before how lonely a motel room could be."

Gem's trembling lips curved into a soft smile as she leaned back against the pillow. "I'd love to be there," she said with simple truth. "I could . . ." She started to say she could come and join him if he would permit it, but Roan interrupted her, his voice back to normal.

"Sorry, honey, but someone's at the door. I'll have to hang up now."

Gem shot upright as her fevered imagination caught at his words, and she was awash in jealous speculation as to who could be knocking at Roan's motel door at this time of night. She remembered all too clearly how successful he could be at seducing a total stranger after a very brief acquaintance. "All right," she gritted out, just keeping her voice from showing her suspicion. "Good night, Roan."

"Good night, babe," Roan said, rather absently, it seemed to Gem, and then the connection was broken and Gem held the phone out in front of her to glare down at the receiver as though it were personally responsible for her present raging feelings.

For the rest of the night Gem tossed and turned in an agony of jealousy, while several hundred miles away the man she loved did the same, though she was unaware of it and would scarcely have believed it had she been told. But Roan's sleep had fled from him as surely as had Gem's upon hearing that she had spent the evening with Billy Martin, and it was a very surly Roan Christianson who set out the next morning to try to convince a suspicious farmer that the man should give him a lease on a pasture the farmer had heretofore considered good only for grazing cows.

CHAPTER FOURTEEN

Gem and Billy worked together as compatibly as though they had been doing so for years, each sparking off the other's creativity and both thoroughly enjoying their sessions, which they seemed to draw out much longer than was strictly necessary to get the job done.

Billy made no reference to his kiss or his statements on the night they had gone out together, and his restraint made Gem more and more fond of him. She was saddened when he had to leave on a concert tour around the country.

He eyed her perceptively as she escorted him to the door on their last day together. "Want me to call you while I'm gone?" he asked casually.

Gem lifted woebegone gray eyes to his, and their sadness diminished slightly at his suggestion. "Would you, Billy?" she asked almost eagerly. "Won't you be too busy?"

"I'll never be too busy for you, darlin'," he teased only half-humorously as he lifted her chin with one finger and brushed her lips with his. "You're my favorite girl, don't you know that?"

Gem sensed the seriousness behind his teasing, but she elected not to acknowledge it. What point would there be in it when she was entangled in her violent emotions for Roan? "Thanks, Billy. For such a bad hero, you make an awfully good friend," she said with a sober smile and teasing eyes.

"Don't be too sure I'm such a bad hero, darlin'," he said with a glint of steel in his blue eyes. "For the right woman I can be as courageous as Tarzan if I have to be. You just asked me to rescue the wrong woman."

Electing to keep things light, Gem folded her hands femininely at her breast and batted her eyes adoringly at him. "Oh, sir," she fluttered in mock confusion, casting her eyes down demurely. "You mean you'd go up against Black Bart bare-handed for little ole me?"

An instant of silence later she raised her eyes to find Billy gazing down at her in a lazy, hooded fashion that reminded her of Roan when he was at his most dangerous. "I'd even go up against Roan Christianson for you," Billy drawled with complete seriousness. "All you'd ever have to do is say the word."

Gem stared up at him, barely having time to close her mouth before Billy's head swooped down to catch her lips in a scorching kiss that shook her to her toes . . . especially when he raised one finger to gently pry her mouth open to receive his tongue before he finished the kiss with no holds barred. When he raised his head to stare into Gem's wide open, rather glazed gray eyes, he was no longer the easy, relaxed, cheerful Billy Martin she had come to know and adore, but a man almost as compelling as Roan.

"I'm not normally a patient man, honey," he growled in a low voice. "But for you I'll wait until you're either married or dead." And with that promise ringing in her ears Gem watched him snatch up his hat and leave her standing there wondering with a nervous little shiver just how she managed to attract men who were so completely . . . male.

With Billy gone Gem couldn't stand the empty house a second longer, and she ran up the stairs to pack a few things, then threw them into her trusty green pickup and set out for her parents' ranch as though the devil were at her heels.

Two days later, after an exhausting round of horseback riding, swimming, and hiking over the gently rolling pastures, she was feeling much more relaxed, but her loneliness was ever present. She hadn't seen Roan for three weeks now, the longest they had been apart since she had come to live with him, and she felt as though half of her were missing.

Her dad, she knew, longed to talk to her about ending her relationship with Roan, but so far he had wisely elected not to do so. Gem thought about telling him she was coming more and more to the conclusion that he would soon have his wish, but something held her back as she stubbornly clung to the hope that she was wrong. But Roan's continued absence and his brief, unsatisfactory phone calls began to convince her that she was wrong to hope.

The brightest spot in her visit was that Pedro called to set the date for his wedding the next month, and the family made plans to attend it with Rosita, who was in such a dither about the marriage, she scarcely knew what she was doing from moment to moment.

Gem did manage to have a brief, private conversation with Pedro after everyone else had had their turn, but she felt even worse at the content of their short discussion.

"How are things going with you and Roan?" Pedro asked with cautious optimism.

Gem hesitated, then gave in to her desire to confide her doubts to someone. "Not very good, Pedro," she sighed. "I think he might be losing interest." She paused, then added, "And I don't know how much longer I can go on living like this, either. It hurts so much to love him, and yet not be able to count on him for . . . for anything."

A short silence greeted her words. "I'm sorry, Gem," Pedro finally said with sad regret. "Perhaps it was wrong of me to encourage you to—"

"No, Pedro!" Gem hastened to reassure him. "Don't blame yourself. I would have done exactly as I did whether I had talked to you about it or not. I had to know, you see. I had to find out if Roan and I could . . ." Her voice trailed off, and she shrugged helplessly. "And the strange thing about it, Pedro," she added with truthful sadness, "is that I don't regret taking the chance.

These past months have been worth whatever I had to go through to get over him."

"Are you so sure it's hopeless, Gem?" Pedro asked sympathetically. "Has he said or done anything to make you certain he no longer wants you?"

Gem didn't know how to answer that. How does one explain intuition? she wondered sadly. "I suppose you could term it benevolent neglect, Pedro," she finally answered. "But it's more than just *his* actions. *I'm* becoming less and less satisfied with the little he can give."

"Yes, I understand, Gem," Pedro answered. "You were never meant for the position you find yourself in now. You deserve more . . . and any woman needs more."

"Yes," Gem said with thoughtful realization, thinking of what Pedro was willing to give his wife-to-be. Love, commitment, loyalty . . . fidelity. "Yes, I do need more," she said with growing determination in her voice. "And I *do* deserve more, don't I?"

"Of course," Pedro answered softly. "But you've always known that."

"I suppose I have," Gem answered thoughtfully. "But he never promised me anything different than what's happening, you know. He spelled everything out clearly from the beginning. It's just that I hoped I could make him see what is possible between two people when they make a commitment. It may have been foolish, but it was worth taking the chance. I suppose I didn't realize that Roan just may not be capable of loving anyone."

"Perhaps," Pedro responded doubtfully. And then, "You sound as though you had definitely made up your mind to leave him, Gem. Have you?"

Gem hesitated, then shook her head. "Not yet, Pedro. Not definitely. But unless there's some change soon, and unless it's for the better . . ." She didn't finish her thought, which was that, given Roan's behavior lately, the change could very well be for the worse, which would at least have the effect of making her decision inevitable.

"Well, remember that I am here if you need me, Gem," Pedro offered predictably. "You only have to ask."

Gem smiled with love and gratitude, knowing that she wouldn't do so. Pedro would soon have even more responsibility riding his slim shoulders than he already had, and she didn't intend to add to his burdens. "Thank you, Pedro," she said softly. "I'll remember." Then she forced a note of bright cheerfulness into her voice. "See you next month, hmmm?"

"Right," Pedro agreed, undisguised happiness entering his voice. "You are to be a bridesmaid, you know."

"Yes, and I'm looking forward to it," Gem replied somewhat untruthfully, for no matter how much she wished Pedro happiness, she thought attending a wedding at this point in her life might prove to be somewhat of a strain. "Tell Marguerita I can't wait to meet her." And after that the two of them said their good-byes, and Gem stood for a while contemplating her own future with a mixture of sadness and resignation.

After another few days at the ranch Gem's increasing restlessness drove her back to the city, though she dreaded facing Roan's empty house again on her own. Once there, she threw herself into a round of appointments—with her hairdresser, to see old friends, shopping, anything she could think of to ease her restless loneliness. But the nights were long and getting longer, and one night she settled down in front of the television set with some light reading, hoping one or the other would hold her interest.

Neither did, however, and she was therefore delighted when the phone rang, and only slightly disappointed when it turned out to be Billy rather than Roan. Roan's phone calls lately left her more depressed than uplifted, and she was as far down tonight as she wanted to go.

"Billy!" she cried delightedly upon learning it was he. "How's the tour going?"

"Outstandingly, from a professional viewpoint," he said in his laconic drawl. "Personally? Well, that's another story."

"What's wrong?" Gem asked anxiously, forgetting for the

moment that Billy's personal difficulties might be connected with herself.

He chuckled wryly. "Come on, Gem, use your imagination. That last kiss didn't do much for my peace of mind . . . or for my sleeping habits."

"Oh." Gem didn't know what else to say, and she was relieved when Billy acknowledged her discomfort.

"Okay, okay." he sighed resignedly. "We won't talk about it . . . yet." Then before Gem could respond to that, he went on to tell her about his tour, and she became caught up in savoring his success vicariously. They talked for quite some time until Gem began to get alarmed at the size of Billy's telephone bill, since he was calling from California.

"Hey, I'm not exactly a pauper, you know," Billy said with a laugh when Gem expressed her concern. "I think I can afford a few bucks for something as pleasurable as talking to you."

"Thanks, Billy," Gem said, "but a fool and his money are soon parted, you know."

"Hmmm." Billy obviously disagreed. "This particular fool is willing to take that chance." Nevertheless, he did soon ring off, and Gem had no more than replaced the receiver when it rang again under her hand.

"Hello?" she asked, wondering if Billy could possibly be calling back for some reason even as she realized he wouldn't have had time.

"Gem . . . this is Roan." He sounded grim, and Gem's sudden rush of joy at hearing his voice died away. It went for good when Roan asked harshly, "Who the hell have you been talking to? I've been trying to get you for an hour."

Her hackles rose at Roan's anger when she had so often waited beside the phone for a call that never came, and her voice was sharper than usual when she answered. "Billy," she responded shortly. "He's on tour, and he called to tell me about it."

She would have quailed if she could have seen the savage look of anger on Roan's face at the information she provided, but it was evident in his voice when he replied anyway. "Quite attentive, isn't he?" he snarled. "Did he by any chance ask you to join him on this tour?"

"No, he didn't!" Gem said angrily in her turn. "And I wouldn't have even if he had! What did you call for, anyway? Just to bawl me out for imagined sins?"

There was a short, sharp silence, then Roan replied more levelly, "No, I called to tell you I'll be home in a week. Will that fit in with your plans?" he drawled with just a tinge of sarcasm.

"What difference would it make if it did?" Gem responded with cold impatience. "This relationship is conducted your way, remember?"

"What does that mean?" Roan asked with a frown in his voice.

"It means no ties, no commitment, no rights," Gem said succinctly. "Except that that only applies one way. I have no doubt that if I did have other plans, you'd change them for me if you felt like it."

"What the hell's the matter with you?" Roan burst out. "You sound like a nagging wife all of a sudden!"

Gem froze at that, and her voice was deadly sweet when she answered. "Oh, never that, surely, darling Roan. Don't be concerned that I've forgotten the rules. You don't have to spell it all out for me again, I've committed your spiel to heart, and I'm not *ever likely to forget it!*" And with that she slammed the phone down in its cradle, clasping a hand over her mouth to stifle the tears that threatened to choke her, and ran to her . . . their . . . bedroom to throw herself down on the bed and indulge in a fit of weeping that had been coming on for days and which she had stifled as long as she was able.

She jumped when the phone shrilled again, then let it ring. After a while it stopped, and she knew the housekeeper had probably picked it up. A few moments later her deduction proved correct when a soft knock came at her door.

"Miss Reasoner," the elderly Mrs. Forrest called. "Mr. Christianson wants to speak to you on the phone."

"You can tell Mr. Christianson to go to—" Gem bit off her words, knowing they would shock the woman and realizing it would do little good to give her such a message since she was unlikely to relay it to Roan anyway. Instead she called, "Tell him I'm not feeling well, Mrs. Forrest. If he wants to call back tomorrow, I'll talk to him then."

She heard the woman hesitating outside the door, then departing, and she rolled over onto her back, contemplating the bleakness of her future with dull eyes and an emptiness in her soul. She had to face it, Gem told herself, straining for the fortitude she needed. Even if Roan weren't tiring of her, which she was certain he was, she was becoming increasingly tired herself . . . tired of uncertainty, tired of the insecurity of her position, and most of all, tired of living a one-sided, unfulfilling love affair.

CHAPTER FIFTEEN

While Gem was desultorily considering her options for the future, Roan was setting about speeding up his return home to the best of his ability. It had taken all his considerable willpower to stay away as long as he had, and he had done it not only for business reasons but to prove to himself that he *could* stay away from Gem without suffering the pangs of the damned in his need for her.

He had been partially successful during the long days while he had been caught up in his business dealings, but entirely unsuccessful during the longer nights when he wanted her soft, pliant body next to him with such an aching need that his self-condemnatory curses had often rung softly through his lonely succession of motel rooms, and each motel's water bills showed a sudden jump during his stays as he took long, unfulfilling cold showers.

Now his patience had run out. A hundred times during his absence he had found himself reaching for the telephone just to hear her voice, and more often than not he had drawn back his hand as if scalded, his countenance twisted with the effort to deny his desire. On the preceding evening he had given in, having had a plausible excuse to do so, and he had fully expected to hear Gem's soft voice ring with happiness at learning he would soon be home. He had been shattered, more than he would allow himself to admit, when she had greeted the news with anger and a decided lack of enthusiasm.

"Damn her!" he cursed grimly as he drove along the lonely road in the beautiful Montana countryside seeking an out-of-the-way ranch. He resented wholeheartedly her advent into his heretofore satisfactory life, bringing with her sleepless nights, a helpless feeling of being subject to someone else's control, and an inability to get her out of his thoughts even in the midst of crucial negotiations when the business at hand demanded his full attention.

But even as he cursed her Roan was picturing her beautiful, serene face in sleep, the childish way she curled her hand against her cheek, the joy and love in her eyes when she saw him at the end of a long, hard day. Even more compelling was his memory of the way she felt in his arms when she was in the throes of passion, the clouded, drugged vulnerability in her clear gray eyes, the husky sound of her voice as she called his name during their lovemaking.

She was like a drug, he thought with self-disgust at his weakness for her. She had gotten into his system, addicted him, and refused to give him any peace from her sorcery. But he goddamned well meant to ride this out until he did have peace of mind again, he thought determinedly as he found the road he sought at last and swung the car onto it. He had no intention of living his life under the influence of someone else, and he was certain—well, almost certain, he admitted with a flash of rare inner truthfulness—that if he gave it time, he could get out from under Gem Reasoner's spell. He was only having a little difficulty with it because she was the first woman he'd ever lived with. Women were insidious with their wiles if you let them get too close, and he was certain it had been a mistake to allow Gem to live with him.

But at the thought of sending her away his face twisted with agony as he pictured his house without her . . . his *bed* without her laughing, loving presence to give his life spice and meaning.

Roan frowned at that last thought. Hell, his life was plenty meaningful, he protested halfheartedly to himself, refusing to acknowledge the bleakness of the last four weeks on the road. Or at least it would be again once he had exorcised Gem from his very guts, he reiterated grimly. He would just give it a little more time. He was sure to get her out of his system if he gave himself the opportunity to live with her just a little longer. Wasn't she already behaving like a shrewish wife, snarling at him like that over the phone?

But his brown eyes were bleak as they traveled unseeingly over country that once would have given him aesthetic satisfaction with its beauty, and all his inner eye saw was Gem's face; all his inner ear heard was the pain in her voice when she had attacked him over the phone the previous evening. And he was glad when he finally sighted the ranch house which was his destination and he could divert his thoughts to something he understood with a clarity that was far from the cloudy, unsettling emotionalism that besieged him whenever he thought of Gem . . . which was far, far too often.

And while he was fighting *his* inner battle Gem was winning her own. With stark realism she knew she had to come to a decision about what to do, and soon. And after long hours of soul-torturing thought she made up her mind. She set a time limit. She would give Roan from the time he arrived home until it was time for her to go to Pedro's wedding in which to take what she offered him so freely. She would devote herself to showing him what love could be like. She would give him every opportunity to return that love. And if he proved incapable of doing so, she would cut her losses and make a new life for herself . . . one that held out the promise of lifelong commitment, mutual love, children, respect, and God willing, the happiness she knew she could give and knew she deserved to receive.

CHAPTER SIXTEEN

On the day Roan was to return, Gem found herself strangely calm, her course set and lending her the fortitude she needed to get through what might turn out to be her last few weeks with Roan. Apart from a slight moistness on her palms and a slightly accelerated heartbeat, she looked the picture of serenity.

For his part Roan, as he pulled into the driveway of his home, was anything *but* serene, and the fact irritated him. His palms, too, were moist, his heartbeat accelerated, and much to his disgust he found his manhood stirring even as he pulled his car to a stop before the steps leading to the front door.

Still, though he resented the physical signs that spelled out his eagerness to be with Gem again and to touch her, he was in no mood to fight them. He would worry later about his threatened independence, after he had possessed his woman once again. A wry smile flicked his lips as he found himself designating Gem as *his woman* in his own mind. But for the moment that indication, too, of her encroachment into his emotions failed to still his impatience as he climbed from the car and hurried up the front steps to enter his home, which, strangely enough, he now designated as "ours" instead of "mine."

"Gem!" he found himself calling even as the door closed behind him, his hand at his tie to loosen it and unfasten the top button of his shirt.

She came down the hallway to greet him, her step unhurried but somehow denoting eagerness even so. Roan's eyes fastened onto her as if glued as he watched her graceful walk making the folds of her full white skirt flutter enticingly around her knees. The silk of her navy blouse clung to her small, uptilted breasts delectably, and the long slender lines of her smooth throat made him ache to kiss it. Her full, tender, softly pink mouth was curved into a welcoming smile, and her large gray eyes were luminescent with welcome and love and a serenity that glowed and enfolded him enchantingly into her presence.

"Roan . . ." she said in her soft, husky, sense-pleasing voice as she came to a stop in front of him and gazed up into his brown eyes with sweet anticipation. "I'm glad you're home," she said simply, and suddenly he was overwhelmingly glad he was too. He found himself saying so without volition, his deep voice conveying his sincerity.

"So am I, baby," he husked as his hands slowly came up to her shoulders. "So am I."

He held back the urge to crush her to him, instead drawing her to his body with slow gentleness, sliding his warm, strong hands down over her shoulder blades and then to her waist, as though he held something too fragile and precious to handle roughly. His enveloping mouth was tender, tasting as he lowered his head for his homecoming kiss, a slight shudder rippling his muscles as he felt her lips open to his and her small, delightful tongue come to meet his with gut-wrenching welcome.

For long, timeless moments they savored each other, enjoying relearning the feel of each other's bodies, touching with hesitant hands and mouths, limbs and muscles, all over, each content to become reacquainted slowly before they reached for the passion that quivered between them.

At last Roan could stand the exquisite torture no longer, and he bent to lift Gem into his arms, starting toward the stairway to their bedroom, his dark eyes speaking to her of his need, drinking in the echo of that need he saw in Gem's.

"You don't have to go to the office?" she asked on a breath so soft he could barely hear her.

He shook his head in the negative. "I don't have to do anything but make love to you," he replied, and the way he said it made it seem as though it was a case of necessity, not choice.

"I'm glad," Gem said simply, raising her head slightly to kiss the planes of his strong, rugged face above her.

Roan's eyes drooped half-closed at the feel of her soft lips feathering his cheek, a slight male smile of acknowledgment lifting one corner of his mouth as he felt himself surge with arousal at Gem's touch.

He undressed her slowly, his eyes deepening, darkening with concentration as he revealed her familiar but ever exciting form to his gaze. "You're as beautiful as ever," he murmured abstractedly, running his hands assessingly over her smooth skin from shoulder to thigh, then back up to her now quivering stomach. "I've missed you, needed you . . ." He bent to place his warm mouth on the lovely lines of her neck, feeling her swallow down a shudder, reveling in that indication of her disturbance.

"I've missed you too," she said with a soft, indrawn breath. "I want to see you."

He drew back slightly to allow her to fumble open the buttons of his shirt, saw her eyes deepen to the darkness of storm clouds as she looked at the male chest she revealed, then felt her trembling touch on him and almost lost control of the urge to crush her to him. He held himself rigid as she unfastened his belt, then his trousers, shuddered as her knuckles brushed his manhood as she unzipped his pants.

Then he watched with almost awed incredulity as she knelt before him to divest him of those pants and almost stumbled as he stepped out of them. Then she was resting her head against his swollen groin, holding his hips with her soft, womanly hands as she nuzzled there, inflaming him unbearably.

His hands trembled as he reached down to draw her to her feet, and he buried his face in her neck and wrapped her into him from shoulder to knee. "My control is shaky," he whispered in an aching voice. "And just when I want it the most. I'm in no mood to hurry."

Gem smiled dreamily, her hands stroking through his thick

hair, then down over his muscled, bunched shoulders. "I'd help you if I could," she murmured sensuously. "But it's been too long for me too."

Roan backed her to the bed then, followed her down to lie side by side as he took another inventory with eyes and hands and mouth of what was his to have whenever he liked. "You're in my soul," he moaned against her breast in a low-voiced shaken tone. "How do I get you out?"

He didn't see the cloudy, saddened look come into Gem's eyes. All he heard was her low croon of sympathetic understanding. "You don't have to, Roan. Not yet."

He felt a relieved satisfaction at hearing her voice say what he wanted to hear. No, he didn't have to get her out of his mind and heart and soul and body yet. She was his for as long as he wanted her. And suddenly, for the first time, he found himself relaxing with the thought that he might want her for far longer than he had planned in the beginning.

That relaxation brought him the control he sought, and his loving was confident, thorough, long, and soul-satisfyingly good for both of them. Gem was content to bank her passion in favor of mutual, tantalizing exploration. She wanted to know every inch of Roan's body with her eyes and hands and body. She implanted him into her memory with deliberate purpose, so that she might recall those memories if they came to be all she had of him. Deliberately she made of herself an instrument of pleasure, thereby pleasing herself, and she was doubly rewarded by Roan's unrestrained appreciation of what she gave him.

Afterward she lay watching him through half-closed eyes, smiling at the relaxation in his limbs and in his normally so alert features. She cuddled him against her, trying to accept the fact that he might have emotional limitations that were not his fault, though it saddened her unbearably when she thought of what they could have together if that weren't true. Then she chuckled as his stomach growled, interrupting her thoughts with vivid, mundane reality.

"Do you want something to eat?" she asked indulgently.

He shook his head languidly, his sensuous mouth curving into a lazy smile. "No," he said in sleepy tones. "I'd have to get up for it, and I'd rather lie here with you for the next twenty-four hours. It's so peaceful."

Gem stroked a lazy finger over his chest, her mouth sliding into a womanly smile. "If we stay here for twenty-four hours," she informed him teasingly, "I have a feeling the peace would be interrupted periodically."

"Naturally." He grinned his contentment. "We have four weeks to make up for."

Gem sat up then, giving a long stretch while Roan watched with possessive enjoyment. "I'll get you something and bring it up here," she said, reaching back to cup his cheek in a spontaneous, loving gesture.

"You don't have to," Roan protested with no real force.

"I know," Gem said simply as she got to her feet. "I want to."

She felt Roan's eyes on her all the while she padded to the closet to fetch a robe and slippers, and then heard his voice teasing her. "If you go down like that, the servants are going to guess what we're up to."

"I wouldn't care if they did," she said, giving a feminine shrug, "but as it happens, I gave them the day off."

Roan's sly grin approved. "Good for you." He nodded, then gave a big yawn. "Hurry back," he said drowsily. "I want you here with me."

His eyes were closed as Gem looked over her shoulder at him, wishing in a far-off, unurgent fashion that his statement were more long-range than immediate but afraid to hope so soon. With a mental shrug she let the thought die and slipped out of the room to go downstairs and fix him a sandwich.

She almost didn't have the heart to wake him to eat it when she brought it back, but as she sat on the bed beside him his eyes came open and he looked at her with the sweetest, most affectionate smile she'd ever had from him. "Thanks," he mumbled as he made the effort to sit up and take the tray from her.

She had fixed enough for both of them, though she wasn't

really hungry, and she barely nibbled as she watched Roan wolf down his food. When he was done, she reached to take the tray and set it beside the bed, and even as she bent over to do it Roan's hands were reaching for her to pull her back to him.

She cuddled beside him, thinking he would want to go back to sleep, then smiled as she felt his hands tugging at her robe to open it. "Take that off," he mumbled as the folds temporarily defeated him. "I'm all thumbs for some reason."

Gem sat up, shrugged out of the robe, and was about to lie down again when Roan came to a sitting position behind her, enchanted by the smooth silkiness of her back. "Bend forward," he instructed quietly. She did so, and then his warm searching lips were at the nape of her neck, then on her shoulders, then feathering down her spine.

"Ahhhh . . ." Gem's sigh was accompanied by a slight shiver of pleasure across the muscles of her back.

"You like that, do you?" Roan's muffled voice came from her waist.

"Very much," Gem said languidly.

"Lie down on your stomach, then," Roan instructed, gently helping to position her as he wanted her, "and I'll do a thorough job of it."

Drowsy enchantment enfolded her as Gem stretched, spread-eagle, on her stomach while Roan feathered every inch of her skin with his lips, occasionally taking erotic little nips that woke her from her semitrance. He reached her delicate, arched feet, then started back up again, and when he arrived at the cleft separating the curved firmness of her feminine buttocks, a sudden liquid swipe of his warm tongue brought her eyes open with a startled gasp.

He chuckled from deep in his throat, then turned her over to gaze down at her from heated eyes. "Time for this side," he said with a quirk of his beautiful mouth.

"Lovely," Gem murmured, raising her arms over her head in a long, voluptuous stretch.

"You lazy little wretch, you're content to lie there all night and let me wash you with my tongue, aren't you?" Roan chuckled, leaning across her to swoop down on her vulnerable throat.

"There's a water shortage . . . I think," Gem mumbled contentedly. "I regard this as your ecological duty."

"Hmmm." Roan snorted against her throat. "If that's the case, then when I'm finished, you'll want to do your duty, too, won't you?" he asked suggestively.

"Love to," Gem agreed without a hint of demurral.

Roan raised his head then, gazing down at her with a combination of lazy arousal, speculative interest, and total appreciation. "I've made you into a perfect bedmate, did you know that, little hedonist?"

Gem's gray eyes fluttered open to return his look with gentle amusement. "Is that what I am now?" she asked interestedly. "A perfect bedmate?" It took effort to keep her desire for other designations, such as wife, mother, friend, from her tone, but she managed it.

"Completely," Roan muttered, his arousal lowering his tone, his body beginning to react more strongly to what rested beneath his hands.

"Well"—Gem gave a languid shrug—"if that's what you've made me, you're entitled to enjoy what you've created. Are you going to?" An arched eyebrow invited him to do just that.

"Thoroughly . . . and at great length," was Roan's reply, given against Gem's softened, parted lips. And then he crushed those lips beneath his own, his hunger overriding his desire to savor at leisure his creation, overtaking his control in a sudden rush of savage passion that swept Gem along into it until they were once again straining, together, for the ultimate peak of ecstasy they knew was waiting to be had.

CHAPTER SEVENTEEN

For those few weeks Roan had nothing from Gem but the utmost in loving, cooperative, accepting, passionate devotion. He responded by becoming more and more deeply enmeshed in the sheer charm of what she gave him, finding himself calling during the day from the office, hurrying home from work, unwilling to accept social invitations because they meant sharing her with others.

Knowingly, with little of his former reluctance, he let himself sink into what he still felt, deep within his subconscious, was an emotional trap, but it was a trap he had lost his taste for resisting . . . not when its walls were silken, it odor exotic, its very atmosphere headily satisfying.

For her part, since Roan took all she gave without once voicing his feelings and with his usual evasion when she even hinted at talk of marriage, love, and children, Gem began to prepare herself emotionally to leave him. There were times when she felt such agony, she didn't know if she could bear it. At other times she felt numbed and dead inside. But whatever her emotional state, her purpose held firm. She would not live like this indefinitely. She would not continue to give all and receive nothing but Roan's body in return. And so she began to lay the groundwork for her departure, her heart torn when Roan's protests were not the jealous, possessive ones of the past, but rather a somewhat forlorn anticipation of loneliness during her absence, which, so far as he knew, would only be temporary.

"But I have to go to Pedro's wedding," Gem said with gentle

persistence one evening at dinner. "I'm going to be a bridesmaid, and Pedro is my oldest friend. I can't let him down."

Roan frowned stubbornly. He had grown used to Gem's acquiesence to his slightest wish, and he had no desire to come home to an empty house for the three days she would be gone. "I wouldn't mind if I could go with you," he said now. "But I have meetings to attend on those days. There'll be no one to go with you."

His flimsy excuse for not coming made Gem smile to herself, secretly, sadly. "Yes, there will," she said quietly. "My parents and Rosita are going. We planned for all of us to go together."

Roan looked positively sulky at that, his features resembling nothing so much as those of a small boy who had been left out of something. Gem reached over to take his hand in hers. "Roan, darling . . ." The endearment slipped out unconsciously, and with her eyes down studying their two hands she didn't see first a look of startlement come into Roan's eyes and then one of pleasure. It was the first time he had heard that word addressed to him from her lips. "Please understand," Gem coaxed. "I *must* do this."

At that moment he might have given her anything she asked for, so strongly did he react to one simple word, spoken with sincerity by a woman who had managed to entwine herself in his life. He hid his own inner confusion at his reaction to such a little thing with humor.

"Call me darling again, and I'll give you the crown jewels," he joked, stirring uneasily when Gem raised surprised gray eyes to his. "All right," he said brusquely. "If you must, you must. But . . ." He stopped, cutting off the admonition he was about to give her to hurry home to him.

"Thank you . . . darling," Gem teased him mistily, unaware of the reason for the slight flush of color that rose in Roan's angular cheeks.

"I suppose you'd better wear Pedro's necklace instead of mine to the wedding," Roan said then, gruffly. Gem blinked at him warily, and he gave her a sardonic smile. "Oh, yes, I know you still have it. I saw you pick it up that day in the motel room in Midland when you thought I wasn't looking."

"Roan, I . . ." Gem started to explain again about the relationship she and Pedro shared, but Roan cut her off.

"Never mind," he said with a roguish smile. "Since Pedro is getting married, I don't consider him competition anymore . . . but you might refrain from telling his *wife* where that necklace came from. She might not be so understanding."

Gem shrugged, a look of sadness coming into her gray eyes. "She would have no reason to be jealous," she said, as if speaking her thoughts aloud, forgetting Roan was there to hear them. "She'll have a plain, solid gold wedding band, and that beats diamonds and emeralds anytime."

She became aware of Roan's rather puzzled and withdrawn look then and cursed herself for not watching her tongue. She forced a cheerful smile onto her face. "How was your day today?" she asked, smilingly changing the subject. And after a moment Roan fell in with her effort, finding in the process, as he had begun to do more and more often these days, that the ability to discuss what he did for a living with someone who cared about hearing it increased his usual pleasure in his work considerably.

On the evening before Gem was to leave Roan for good, she finished her packing with trembling fingers, hoping Roan wouldn't notice that she was taking with her far more than would normally be necessary for a three-day trip. If he did notice, she planned to make some vague, feminine excuse about not being able to make up her mind about what to wear and being prepared for anything.

To please him, she wore his gift of the diamond and emerald earrings and necklace to dinner, and even to bed that night. "Hey," he teased as he came to join her and shrugged off his robe, exposing his magnificent, newly showered male body to her longing eyes, "are jewels and nudity the 'in' thing to wear to bed these days?" But his teasing failed to hide the real pleasure he took in her gesture, and Gem was glad she had thought to make it.

"Of course," she tossed back lightly, adopting a languid, regal pose and a haughty expression. "One never knows when a fashion photographer may burst into the bedroom, and it pays to be prepared."

Roan's look was possessively sardonic as he lay down beside her. "Don't count on it," he growled, taking her into his arms, "because I made sure to lock the door. If I'm going to have to do without you for three days, I want to fortify myself against the coming famine."

"How nice," Gem murmured, wrapping her arms about him and accommodating herself to his curves and hollows familiarly. "That's exactly what *I* had in mind." And then she hid her face in his shoulder to conceal the fact that her heart was breaking with the knowledge that the famine he spoke of, on her part at least, was going to last a lifetime. Roan's, she knew, would last only until he found someone to replace her in his bed . . . and then someone else, and another, and another, until he ended his life alone, just as he preferred.

She stored up memories that night, surprising, pleasing, and puzzling Roan with the urgency and passion she displayed, going even so far as to wake him from sleep twice, something she had never done before. He took what was given with all of Gem's love, eagerly, and with an enjoyment that spurred her on to new heights of creativity and energy.

The next morning his eyes were ruefully weary as he stood looking down at her as he buttoned his shirt, but there was satisfaction there as well. "Maybe you should go away more often," he growled teasingly, "though I'm not sure I could stand up to your version of good-bye with the stamina you deserve on a regular basis."

Gem smiled faintly, hoping the unhappiness she felt would be misconstrued as weariness rather than sadness. "I'll keep that in mind," she said huskily, "and keep my good-byes to . . . the barest minimum."

"Good," Roan said with quiet satisfaction, failing to note the hesitation or the slight catch in her voice, or if he did, unaware of their cause. He went to his closet for his jacket and tie, and Gem watched every move he made through dilated pupils, drinking in this last sight of him hungrily, an empty ache in her breast where her heart should have been.

"I'll see you in three days, then?" Roan asked as he came back to the bed to lean over her, making a last assessment with his softened brown eyes. Then he chuckled as he noted the tired droop of her passion-swollen lips. "Or are you going to lie in bed all day recuperating and miss the wedding completely?"

Gem shook her head slightly, reaching up a hand to cup his cheek, her eyes roaming his beloved face with a hint of desperation. "Hey," he chided, taking her palm in his hand to kiss it lingeringly. "It's only three days. You're not going away forever, you know."

Gem closed her eyes briefly to conceal her pain at his words, and her voice failed her. So she merely raised her head to press her lips against his cheek lovingly. "Good-bye, darling," she whispered with the throb of tears in her husky voice.

Roan turned his head, captured her mouth for a brief, enveloping kiss, then straightened to gaze down at her with a hint of puzzled though pleased gentleness. "Be careful, sweetheart," he admonished her, low-voiced. "I want you back in one piece."

Gem swallowed, then made the effort to give him a brilliant smile. "You, too, Roan," she said softly. "You take care of yourself too."

"Hell, I'm too mean to get hurt." He grinned at her as he moved toward the door. "It's only softies like you that life bounces around like a rubber ball." He had the door open by now, and his last gesture was a blown kiss, a wink, and a murmured, "So long, honey. Hurry back." And then he was gone, while Gem's eyes remained fixed to the door, where he had seemed to stand for a long while after he was no longer there.

CHAPTER EIGHTEEN

Amidst the noise of cheering and laughter all around her, Gem stood gazing down at the lovely, simple bouquet of pink rosebuds she had caught automatically when it was thrown to her, her lips trembling with heartbreak as she thought how unfair it was that Marguerita should have thrown the flowers to her instead of to someone who might have had a chance at fulfilling the prophecy they represented.

Raising moistened eyes to where Pedro and Marguerita stood smiling warmly at her, she made the effort to appear pleased that she knew Marguerita, if not Pedro, expected. She blew a kiss to the lovely dark girl standing in the circle of Pedro's arm and was rewarded by another shy, gentle smile of affection. Then Gem caught Pedro's warm, sympathetic eyes and winked at him courageously, telling him nonverbally that she would be all right . . . that his new wife's entirely sincere gesture at making sure she, Gem, caught the bouquet was appreciated for its intent, since the girl couldn't know how inappropriate her well-meant gesture really was.

Then everyone was chasing the couple as they dashed to the new little economy car Jim Reasoner had given them as a wedding present, throwing rice, laughing, calling out humorous and sometimes lewd, suggestions, and Gem followed them, grateful when Derek placed his arm around her shoulders to give her a quick hug of understanding. At the last moment she had called him, begging him to come to the wedding with her to help her remain firm in her resolve and to lend her moral support.

"That will be you someday, Gem," Derek whispered fiercely into her ear. "Even if I have to marry you myself."

Relaxing somewhat, Gem gave him a rueful, amused smile. "*Have* to?" she teased him, enjoying his wince as he realized how what he had said must have sounded to her. "Sherri might be glad to hear how you put that," Gem mocked him chidingly, "but it didn't do a thing for *my* ego."

Derek gave her shoulder another reassuring squeeze. "You know I didn't mean it like that, honey," he apologized sheepishly. And then a wicked gleam lit his dark eyes, and he grinned as he looked down at her. "But on the other hand, if we did get married, I'll bet both Sherri and Roan *would* sit up and take notice finally."

Gem attempted a laugh that didn't quite come off. "Yes, I think you could count on it," she agreed quietly, "but from what you've told me, I don't think you have to go to such lengths with Sherri any longer. It sounds like she's coming around. You're just too irresistible to let get away," she finished solemnly.

"Hell, yes!" Derek smirked with mock conceit, but his eyes were gentle as he added, "At least one of us Christianson boys has got the sense we were born with."

Gem lowered her eyes and squeezed his arm. "Hush, Derek. Roan can't help it. It isn't his fault he's like he is."

Derek snorted in disagreement. "Well, he could damned well try to help it, if you ask me," he said gruffly. "And it *is* his fault if he can't recognize a treasure when he sees one." And then his eye grew serious. "I think it's a mistake not to tell him about your leaving, Gem. Maybe it would wake him up to what he's letting get away."

Gem shook her head firmly. "No, Derek. He had his chance. Until you tell him, I don't want him to know I *am* getting away, as you put it. And if you break your promise to me and tell him *where* I'm going, I'll never forgive you. I'm under no illusions that he loves me, but I'm well aware he still wants me. He's fully capable of following me to pressure me into coming back to him, and I can't go through this more than once." Her look became more determined as she saw Derek fidget with impatient disagreement with her reasoning. "*No,* Derek," she reiterated firmly.

"Hell," Derek exploded with exasperated grimness. "You sure know how to tie a guy up in knots, do you know that, Gem Reasoner?"

"No, I didn't know that," Gem responded calmly. "And if I hadn't had complete faith in your friendship, I wouldn't have put you in this position. I'm sorry now I did. It was unfair of me. But . . ."

Derek cut in, his frown stern. "I don't want to hear that," he said with gruff affection. "I told you a long time ago to call on me if you needed me, and I'm proud you did. I just hate to see the two people I love most in the world . . . aside from Sherri," he added with a soft smile, "making a mess of their lives. You and Roan belong together."

A soft bleakness faded the gray in Gem's eyes to slate. "I thought we did, too, Derek, but it seems I was wrong." Then she took a deep breath and straightened her shoulders. "I think we've discussed this enough, Derek. My mind is made up. Please accept my decision. It's my life, and I have to live it my way."

"Whatever you say, Gem," Derek said, conceding defeat. He opened his mouth to say one more thing, but at Gem's soft shaking of her head he desisted. "Okay," he breathed in resignation. "What do you say we leave here and go get drunk on tequila, then?" he asked, his eyes following the dust of the small car Pedro and Marguerita were leaving in.

Gem laughed shortly. "I have the feeling that wouldn't help how I feel right now," she said dryly, "though it's tempting. But I'll go with you to keep you out of trouble if you like," she added teasingly. "That's the least a friend would do, isn't it?"

Derek gave a shrug of his powerful shoulders. "I swear, Gem, I don't know what a friend's supposed to do anymore . . . much less a brother."

"Sure you do," Gem said firmly, taking his arm and pulling him toward her parents to tell them where they were going.

"You just be yourself and care about us. That's all that's required."

Despite Derek's best efforts he never did get inebriated enough for his thoughts to be blotted out, and the next morning, as he helped Gem and her parents load up her pickup for her forthcoming journey, all he had to show for his night of trying were bloodshot eyes and a pounding headache.

Gem hugged her mother good-bye first, grateful that Audra Reasoner showed no sign of disappointment or pity, but rather steady, calm support. She hugged her dad next, wincing as she saw the unhappiness in his gray eyes that she was leaving him again. "Honey, don't you think . . ." he started to say, then stopped as Gem lifted a hand to place her fingers over his lips.

"Don't worry, Daddy," she said lovingly. "I'm a grown woman. I'll be all right. I'll keep you informed constantly of how I am, and you can visit me in Nashville anytime you like." She stepped back and gave him a bright, brave smile. "I'm going to make you very proud of me, Daddy."

Jim Reasoner nodded. "I already am, honey," he said in a choked voice. "I always will be."

Gem turned her misted eyes away from him and gave herself to Derek's arms for a long, fervent bearhug. Finally he held her away from him to gaze at her with sad admiration. "Good-bye, little sister," he murmured, and as he saw the sweet gratitude in her eyes for this designation, he grinned crookedly. "I always did want a sister, anyway," he murmured gruffly. "And if I can't have one legally, I'll just adopt one without benefit of the law."

Gem nodded, swallowing down her tears. "Good-bye, brother," she said firmly. "And good luck with Sherri. Let me know how it goes, hmmm?"

He nodded and kissed her on the cheek and then she turned away to climb into the pickup and get started before she broke down in front of them all. She drove away with her tears blurring the scenery around her, but not enough so that she failed to see the identical expressions on the three faces of those who watched her go. All her loved ones were saddened, angry, and to a person afraid for her, hating to let her go alone to face a future without their protection . . . or without the support and love of the man who should have been by her side.

Gem swiped her tears away determinedly, straightening her shoulders and increasing her speed, resolving that she would do her best to keep from hurting those who loved her again, and knowing that the best way she could do that was to make a satisfactory life for herself.

The miles stretched ahead and behind her relentlessly, and she had never felt so alone, but she knew that she had her career, and perhaps someday would have someone to ease that loneliness, and that thought was the only thing that kept her foot to the accelerator and her eyes facing forward toward the future.

CHAPTER NINETEEN

Derek Christianson was prepared to face almost any reaction from his brother when he was told of Gem's departure but the one he got. He stared puzzled and a little alarmed when Roan's face first paled, then went blank, and then his whole body seemed to draw in upon itself for a moment. But when Roan spoke at last, it was in an almost toneless voice.

"Why?"

The one word irritated Derek, both because he felt Roan should have known the answer to his own question, and because Roan's attitude seemed uncaring. He shrugged, and his voice was sharp when he answered. "Why not?" he asked sarcastically. "Did you think she would be content to be your mistress indefinitely? She's got a hell of a lot more to offer some man than that!"

Roan's eyes were hooded and withdrawn as he glanced at his brother obliquely. Then he shrugged his powerful shoulders and turned away. "If you say so," he said in that same toneless voice, and Derek became so angry, he took a threatening step toward his brother before he caught himself up and stopped, his fists clenched uselessly at his sides.

"You goddamned imbecile," he swore with quiet rage. "If you weren't my brother . . ." He broke off, took a shuddering breath, then turned sharply away to head for the front door. He was afraid if he stayed in Roan's presence one more moment, he would slug him.

Derek's anger might have lessened considerably if he had stayed around to watch Roan climb the stairs to his bedroom with slow, measured steps, his face locked into a stony mask to conceal the pain twisting inside him. Once inside the room he had shared so briefly with Gem, he closed the door behind him, leaned against it, and let his features relax into a contorted landscape of agony. His eyes rested on the bed where Gem had given so freely of her love, and he closed them quickly, a savage grimace twisting his lips into a snarl.

"Bitch!" The word burst from him as he struggled with a sense of loss he had only had to face one other time in his life, when his father died, and then the loss had been expected and was tempered by a different kind of love, not this gut-wrenching, helpless, overwhelming obsession that had taken him unawares, and which gave him no peace.

"Women!" he snarled, thrusting himself away from the door and moving with hard purposefulness toward the closet where Gem had kept her things. There was little left there now, but what there was Roan ripped from the hangers and threw on the bed before finding an old suitcase and thrusting them inside it. He went back to the closet to gather up what shoes Gem had left, failing to notice that one small nearly new sneaker tumbled from his arms and fell into a dark corner of the closet.

After throwing the shoes into the suitcase he went to the dresser Gem had used and tore open the lid of the case in which she had kept her jewelry. Blinking up at him were the earrings and necklace he had given her, and he snatched them up in one fist, raised his arm to sling them at a wall, then stopped, slowly lowering his hand to gaze at the twinkling gems where they lay on his palm. "Goddamn you, Gem," he whispered in a shaken voice. "Goddamn you to hell!"

He stood for long moments staring at what he held, picturing how they had looked at her small, shell-like ears and around her slender, delectable neck on that last night she had spent with him. The image brought moisture to his eyes, the first time that had happened since he was a very small boy indeed, before he had learned to close his emotions away into some dark, forgotten corner of his heart where they couldn't be touched . . . and hurt.

With a sense of shock Roan angrily rubbed the moisture away, then tossed the jewelry back into the case and slammed the lid down. But even as he did so he was remembering that Gem had never seemed to appreciate them anyway. She had seemed far more enamored of that small, inexpensive pendant Pedro had bought her, and envious of the plain gold wedding band her friend would be giving his betrothed.

A hard, slashing smile curved his masculine lips as he rationalized that Gem was just like every other woman he'd ever known—set on trapping some poor, unsuspecting male into marriage so that she could make his life miserable once she had him where she wanted him. He told himself he was *glad* she'd woken up to the fact that he himself was never going to fall into such a trap, and he sneered harshly as he wondered who she would set her cap for next. Billy Martin? But the flash of raging jealousy that shot through him at that thought threatened to break down his hard-held control, and he swung away from the dresser to close and snatch up the suitcase, carrying it purposefully down to the kitchen to thrust it at his housekeeper.

"Get rid of these things, Mrs. Forrest!" he snapped at the wide-eyed, anxious-looking woman. "Miss Reasoner won't be back, and I don't want them around here!" He ignored her open-mouthed astonishment as he turned on his heel to leave the house and drive at an unsafe speed to his office, where he threw himself into his work with an energy that left his secretary drained and complaining by the time he let her go home for the day.

Then, faced with the long, empty hours of the evening and night ahead of him, Roan snatched the phone from the hook and dialed the number of a woman who knew the rules of the game he had played for years and was now determined to return to; one who had as little use as had he for emotional commitment, romantic nonsense, and all the garbage that went with them.

Several hours later he returned to his house, grim-faced with the knowledge that for the first time in his life he had been unable to perform with a woman. With a sharp economy of motion that spelled out his need to get out of the room that held too many memories for him, he threw clothing into a bag, scribbled a note for his housekeeper, and left on an unnecessary business trip that would keep him away long enough to allow him to get Gem's ghostly presence out of his mind, out of his life, and most of all, out of this room, where he fully intended to sleep—alone—for many years to come.

Two weeks later he was back, grimly discouraged to find that the ghost still resided wherever he looked, wherever he went, and he settled down with stoic patience to await the time when such would not be the case. He dated relentlessly, yet found himself avoiding, indeed, unable to contemplate a sexual relationship with any of the many women who were happy to receive his attentions.

He worked hard, long hours, then found himself unable to sleep when he returned home exhausted. He lost weight. His face grew more sharp-planed and haggard. His tone of voice grew harsher. Nothing pleased him . . . nothing and no one. And as the weeks ground by relentlessly his eyes went colder, bleaker . . . lonelier.

Derek saw little of him during this time. He had his own problems to work out, but his were more easily resolved. And at last the day came when he had a solid commitment from Sherri, a date for the wedding had been set, and it occurred to him to inform his brother that his services as best man would be required in the near future.

It was a Sunday, and Derek found Roan slouched in front of a football game on television, looking unshaved, bleary-eyed from the whisky he had drunk already, testified to by the half-empty bottle that stood beside his chair, and in casual, wrinkled clothing that looked slept in.

"Hey, brother," Derek greeted Roan uncertainly, unable to believe the changes he was seeing in his hitherto immaculately dressed, perfectly turned-out sibling. "How are you?"

Roan looked up at him out of eyes grown distant and cold. "I'm fine, Derek," he said in tones only slightly slurred from drink. "What brings you here?" His tone was uncaring, and Derek began to grow alarmed, wondering if Roan were suffering from some illness.

"I'm getting married to Sherri," Derek offered, taking a seat on a nearby sofa and sliding down on his spine. "Thought I'd fill you in on the details. I want you for my best man, you know."

He was shocked by the bitter smile that curved Roan's ravaged mouth. "Fell into the trap finally, did you?" Roan asked disparagingly.

"I don't look at it that way," Derek returned quietly. "I've wanted to marry Sherri since we were kids. You know that."

"Sure." Roan gave a negligent shrug. "You were always a sap for all that garbage."

Derek frowned, his temper flaring in spite of his concern over his brother's appearance. "It's not garbage, Roan," he replied, tight-lipped. "It's about the only damned thing in this whole crazy world that makes any sense."

"Do tell," Roan sneered, reaching a hand down for the liquor bottle and pouring a generous portion into the glass he held. "Well, let's hope you're not disappointed, little brother," he said with an unamused smile. "Women are not known for their faithfulness, in case you haven't noticed."

Derek stared at him for a long moment, a storm of anger growing in his dark eyes. "If you're talking about Gem, you couldn't be more wrong," he said in an ice-cold voice.

Roan seemed to stiffen for a moment, but then he made a visible effort to relax. "What makes you think I'm talking about her," he said dismissively. "I never even think about that little bitch anymore."

"Don't call her a bitch!" Derek snarled, jumping to his feet to pace dangerously to where Roan still sat slouched in his chair. "If you can't show her any respect as a woman, at least admit she left because she loved—" He bit off what he was about to say, drawing back slightly as he saw Roan's eyes suddenly become crystal clear, the cloudy, distant look gone in an instant.

Slowly Roan sat up, looking impressively powerful even in his disheveled state. "Well, go on, brother," he said on a soft, dangerous note. "Exactly why is it I should show Gem any respect when she walked out . . ." He stopped, tightened his lips, and leaned back to watch Derek out of cold, perceptive eyes, which grew more and more alert as he saw Derek adopt the expression he had worn since childhood when he was trying to hide something.

"Forget it, Roan," Derek finally said with beligerent harshness. "You aren't really interested, and even if you were, you don't deserve to . . ." Suddenly Derek shut up. He ran a hand through his thick hair, took a deep breath, blew it out, and paced to the window. "Are you going to be best man at my wedding or not, Roan? That's all I came over here to find out."

Roan ignored the question, as though he hadn't heard it. "Where is Gem, Derek?" he asked in a deceptively soft voice. "You must keep in touch with her. Where is she and what's she doing now?"

Derek wouldn't look at him, and Roan's expression grew sharper. "What do you care, Roan?" Derek said wearily. "Just drop it. Now are you . . ."

Suddenly Roan was on his feet and behind Derek, gripping his shoulder painfully, turning him around. "I asked you a question," he said in a harsh voice with a savage look in his dark eyes that made Derek step back.

"It's none of your business, Roan," Derek said angrily, defensively. "You should have made it your business to find out a long time ago."

Roan's face whitened. "Is she married, then?" he asked in a harsh whisper.

Derek looked at him with disgust. "No, she's not married," he said in a hard voice. "You pretty well broke . . ." Once again he stopped, realizing he was on the verge of saying too much. Then his gaze grew speculative as he saw Roan's expression reveal both anguish and relief for a bare instant before Roan covered up again. After a long silence, wherein Roan turned his back on Derek and returned to his chair to reach for the bottle with a shaking hand, Derek's eyes began to gleam with something like understanding and satisfaction. He quickly concealed that gleam when Roan faced him again, cool challenge replacing it.

"If you want to know where Gem is, you'll have to find her on your own, brother," he said with careful blandness. "That shouldn't be too hard for a man of your intelligence."

Roan's head snapped up. "What is that supposed to mean?" he asked hardly. "And what makes you think I'm interested?"

Derek shrugged. "Think about it," he drawled, his eyes inadvertently swinging to the stereo set on the far wall. "And I didn't say you *were* interested. I said *if* you wanted to find her." He gave an unamused laugh. "I doubt if you have sense enough to be that smart. For a man of intelligence you can be damned stupid at times."

"Thank you for the charming testimonial," Roan clipped coldly. "It's nice to know family loyalty is still alive and thriving."

Derek shook his head, his eyes sad and tired. "You have my loyalty, Roan," he uttered in a tone that matched his expression. "You even have my love. But there have been times when you sure as hell haven't had my respect."

He grabbed up his jacket then, pulling it on impatiently and starting toward the door. He paused there, his hand on the frame, and looked back at where Roan stood, his expression closed.

"I'll get back to you about the wedding plans, Roan. Meanwhile . . ." He paused and raked his brother disgustedly with his eyes. "Meanwhile why don't you give a little thought to why you're going to hell in a hand basket. You're thirty-five years old, for God's sake! Don't you think it's about time you grew up and stopped replaying Dad's life like a tired old movie? I was only fifteen when he died, but if I remember correctly, he was a tired, lonely old man who didn't have anybody in the world but the two of us . . . and we weren't enough, Roan." He shook his head sadly. "No, we just weren't enough . . . and you won't even have that when you go." Then he turned on his heel and walked out, leaving Roan to stare after him, only the muscle moving in his jaw and the bleakness in his eyes showing that his brother's attempt to get through to him had succeeded in any way whatever.

CHAPTER TWENTY

Gem held on to Billy Martin's arm as they were jostled by the crowd backstage at the Grand Old Opry. The performance was over, and everyone was laughing and joking and congratulating one another on a job well done. Another famous star stopped in front of the two of them and slapped Billy on the shoulder.

"Good job, son!" He beamed his congratulations. "You wowed 'em out there tonight." Then his twinkling eyes took in Gem's delectable figure where she stood, looking coolly sophisticated in her long, black velvet evening gown, and the man bowed his head to her. "Is this your wife?" he asked pleasantly.

Billy's mouth curved into a reluctant smile as he looked down at Gem, his eyes regretful. "No, sir," he said calmly. "I haven't been able to talk her into marrying me yet. This is Gem Reasoner. I was singing her songs out there tonight."

The star's eyes widened with respect as he held out his hand for Gem to take. "Well, well," he said admiringly. "I've been wanting to meet you for some time, young lady, and tell you how much I like those songs you've been turning out. I don't suppose you'd consider spreadin' the wealth around and creating something for an older man to sing, would you?" He asked the question lightly, his laughter underlining his teasing.

"Thank you," Gem said with a smile, her blush revealing her slight awe of the famous man who had paid her such a compliment. "I'd love to someday, but I'm pretty well committed right now."

"I'll bet you are, honey," the man said, his eyes sweeping over her lovely face, their blueness gentle with regard. "But if you ever find the time and you come up with something that's my style, just call my agent. You know what my style is, don't you?"

Gem knew he wasn't being immodest, just honest. There was hardly a country and western fan who *didn't* know his style, since his records were played night and day on the radio. "I surely do," she said, gazing at him admiringly. "And I'll remember."

When at last she and Billy were able to leave, Gem gave a sigh of relief. She was tired, her feet hurt, and she wanted her bed. She hated to turn down Billy's invitation to a late supper out somewhere, knowing he needed to wind down after his performance, but she just wasn't up to it.

"You go ahead, Billy," she urged as they crossed the parking lot to his pickup truck. "You can drop me at the apartment and join the others. You don't have to stay with me."

"Gem," Billy said with mocking gentleness. "When I came to town, I was looking forward to seeing you more than I was singing at the Opry. Doesn't that tell you anything?"

Gem ducked her head, knowing exactly what Billy was trying to tell her, but unable to respond as he would like. "Billy, please . . ." she said faintly. "You know I'm not ready . . ."

"I know, babe," Billy said nonchalantly. "I'm not pushing. But if you don't mind, I'm not going to back away from a chance to spend time with you, either. You gonna begrudge me that?"

Gem shook her head no, smiling up at him and in her concentration on Billy failing to note the car parked near Billy's truck or the man who sat behind the wheel, staring at the two of them with a bleakness in his eyes that would have broken her heart if she had seen it.

Back at her small, cheerful apartment Gem fixed Billy a snack, then sat and talked to him for an hour or so before her yawns and drooping eyelids made Billy get determinedly to his feet. "It's time you were in bed," he said gruffly. "I've kept you too long."

"No, you haven't!" Gem protested affectionately. "I'm so glad to see you again, I could talk all night."

"Yes, well, I can't," Billy said somewhat grimly. "I keep wanting to put you to bed, climb in beside you, and love you up. I think I'd better go find some company that doesn't make me wish that torch you're carrying were for me instead of a jerk who's too stupid to know what he threw away."

"Billy . . ." Gem's shadowy eyes reproached him, and he tightened his mouth with regret at his own outspokenness.

"Sorry, honey," he muttered, then made a determined effort to regain his normal cheerfulness. "Hey, I like that song about the little boy and his daddy's truck. You think maybe it's because the kid's name is Billy too?"

Gem laughed and then pouted at him. "No, it's because it's a darned good song," she asserted stoutly. "Anyway," she taunted him mercilessly, "I'm thinking about changing the boy's name from Billy to Teddy. I don't want that family to hear the song and recognize who it's about."

"You wouldn't dare!" Billy scowled ferociously, and then he looked at her in surprise. "You mean that story's true?" he asked interestedly.

"Yep," Gem admitted. "But don't tell anyone. It's my secret."

Billy's expression turned sly. "Okay, I'll promise not to tell if you promise not to change the boy's name. And if you promise I can have the song."

"Oh, Billy, you conceited idiot!" she scolded him in mock anger. "Of course, you can have the song. Even without blackmail!"

Billy grinned his satisfaction, and as they arrived at the door to the apartment he grabbed her shoulders to give her a smacking kiss. But the kiss, which he had started in a moment of exuberance, threatened to become more than an expression of simple affection, and Gem put her hands on his chest to push him gently away. "No, Billy," she whispered sadly.

He stared down at her, frustration in his eyes, and then he smiled forlornly. "Not yet?" he asked coaxingly.

Gem hesitated, not wanting to discourage him completely, though she knew it might be a very long time before she could push Roan's memory away to the extent that she could tolerate another man's embrace. "No, not yet, Billy," she temporized.

Billy cupped her face and leaned down to kiss her forehead gently. "Well, at least you didn't say not ever," he said softly, causing Gem to feel guilty at giving him some hope.

"Billy, you shouldn't wait for me," she said with anxious sadness in her gray eyes. "Find someone else, Billy. It may be a long time before . . ."

"I told you once," he cut in, "that I'd wait until you were either married or dead. That's the way it still stands, kid." He shrugged fatalistically. "You know what I'm talking about. You're still carrying a torch yourself, aren't you?"

Gem lowered her eyes, hesitated, then nodded with a bare jerk of her head.

"Ah, well." Billy sighed, reaching for the doorknob behind him. "If there weren't situations like this all the time, there'd be no need for sad songs, would there?" He flashed his charming smile at her as Gem acknowledged the truth of his statement. "I'll see you tomorrow, okay?"

"Okay," Gem agreed, smiling affectionately at him.

When he was gone, Gem trailed tiredly into her bedroom, slipped off her clothes, and donned a soft, silky pink nightgown that made her skin glow with life. She pulled a brush through her long hair, her lids drooping at the hypnotic motion, then was jarred into alertness by the sound of a knock at the door of the apartment.

Frowning, wondering if it were Billy again and feeling guilty at hoping that it was not, Gem slipped on a matching robe and padded to the front door. She peeked through the small circle of glass in the door, then gasped, her heart missing a beat as she recognized Roan's tall frame standing outside.

"Oh, God!" she murmured to herself, closing her eyes and resting her head against the wooden panel of the door. The mere sight of him, distorted as it was through the glass, still had the power to turn her to jelly, and she knew if she let him in, she would never be able to resist if he wanted her.

The knock came again, and then Roan's low voice, speaking as though he knew she was just on the other side of the door. "Open up, Gem," he said in a low, ragged tone. "Let me in."

Gulping down her panic, Gem bit her lip, started to tell him to come back the next day, then realized that wouldn't solve anything. He would. And she would still be faced with her overwhelming reaction to his presence.

"Gem!" The urgency and determination in his voice as he called her name made Gem realize she was going to have no choice even as he told her so. "Don't be afraid of me, Gem," he urged. "I have to see you. I'll stand here all night if I have to."

Gem blinked at that, surprised at some note in his voice she had never heard before. He sounded despairing, pleading even, but definitely determined. In response to that tone she found her hands moving to the lock of the door, and as the soft click signaled its release the door was pushed inward as Roan acted swiftly to gain entrance.

Gem stepped back as he came across the threshhold, her eyes flying to his face, then darkening with pain as she saw his gauntness, the burning look of weary anguish in his dark eyes, the lines of suffering in his forehead and down his cheeks.

"Roan!" she cried softly. "Have you been ill?" The loving concern and vicarious pain were audible in her voice.

Roan stood taking all of her in with his deep brown eyes darkening to velvet, devouring her with his gaze, his expression softening as he saw the anxiety on her face. He shook his head as if clearing it before he finally spoke. "No, honey, I haven't been sick. Not physically, at least. Just in my soul."

Gem's gray eyes widened in puzzlement, her soft mouth trembling with the desire to kiss away his trouble. "I don't understand," she said with soft helplessness.

"I didn't either," he said on a deep note of emotion. "Not until you left me. And even then it took awhile of living in hell before

I realized you and Derek were right all along. Loving is the only thing that makes any sense in this empty world."

Gem unconsciously drew back a step, incapable of believing that Roan could have changed so drastically. He misinterpreted her movement, and his face contorted with pain as he asked the question that was eating him alive. "Am I too late?" he almost whispered. "Are you in love with Billy now?" His eyes burned into her as he added, "I couldn't stand it if that were true, Gem. When I saw you with him tonight, I almost . . ."

Gem broke in in surprise. "You saw us tonight?"

Roan's nod was impatient and grim. "I came here first, and one of your neighbors told me where you were, so I went looking for you. I've been looking for you all my life, Gem. I just didn't know it."

Gem closed her eyes, strengthening herself against giving in to the joy that was threatening to flood her senses in case what Roan seemed to be telling her turned out not to be true. She jumped when she felt him come to within a breath of her, then shuddered as he gently took her face into his hands. "Do you love Billy, Gem?" he asked in an agonized whisper.

Seemingly of its own volition she found her head shaking its denial. "Then do you love me?" he asked almost humbly, his voice shaking with his need.

At last she opened her eyes to stare up at him, giving him her answer before her lips formed the words. "Yes," she whispered. "Always."

He pulled her into his arms then, holding her so tightly she found it hard to draw breath. "Keep loving me, Gem!" he begged, his voice muffled against her throat. "Don't ever stop! Don't ever leave me again! I love you, Gem! I love you!"

Gem clung to him, believing his tone even more than his words. She tried to tell him with her body what he wanted to hear, her voice too choked with tears to speak. But when he lifted his head to gaze down at her, asking without words for her promise, she found her voice.

"I will, Roan," she whispered tremulously. "I'll never stop loving you. I'll never leave you. I promise, darling . . . I promise."

His lips trembled when he kissed her, as did Gem's, but it was by far the best kiss she had ever received from him, for it was the first kiss he'd ever given her out of love. When he drew back, they looked at one another hungrily, Roan's eyes tenderly devouring, Gem's shining with the emotion she was starved to show openly.

"Do you want to get married here or in Texas?" Roan asked in a deep, emotion-ridden voice.

Gem considered that, wanting to become his as soon as possible, but then, realizing she was already his, and there was no need for quite so much urgency, she smiled her love. "In Texas," she said. "My father has always looked forward to walking down that aisle with me."

Roan nodded, smiling, then stepped back to reach into his pocket. "I've brought you something," he said almost hesitantly. "And I think . . . I hope . . . you'll like it better than you did my last gift."

He brought his hands up between them and opened a small box for her to see. And in it rested *two* plain gold wedding bands, one for him as well as one for her, and Gem stared at them for long seconds before she raised shimmering eyes to his.

"Oh, Roan," she breathed with heartfelt gratitude. "They're so beautiful. Thank you . . . oh, thank you, my darling. Thank you so much!"

He shook his head with a little smile of mocking amazement. "They're not that expensive," he teased gently. "No diamonds . . . no emeralds . . . just plain gold."

"I never wanted diamonds and emeralds from you, my darling," Gem said softly as Roan, refusing to wait, slipped one gold band over her finger, then held out the other ring for Gem to put it on his. "This is all I ever wanted from the first night I met you."

"And I was too much of an idiot to want the same thing," Roan replied, pulling her back into his arms. "God, I'm glad you stuck around to educate me about what's really important in life . . . I'm even glad you left me so that I could find out what it was I really wanted . . . not what I intended."

Gem laughed softly as Roan began to nuzzle her throat, appreciating his tender reminder that he had done the same for her once. "It's only fair, my beautiful Roan," she said, her voice growing lower, huskier as Roan nipped and licked her throat as though he were hungry and needed to be fed. "You taught me what I wanted . . . how to *make* love. So I had to teach you what love is, didn't I?"

"You did that, all right," he said with husky arousal as he picked her up in his arms. "Now how about if we go into the bedroom and put our learning together. I feel sure we haven't taught each other everything there is to know about loving."

"I hope not," she replied, snuggling against him as he moved toward the bedroom. "I'm an insatiable student, and I hate know-it-alls."

He chuckled lovingly as he set her on her feet beside the bed. "I haven't forgotten how you love to learn," he said seductively. "I never forget anything, remember?" And his eyes echoed that thought as he divested her of her robe and then her gown, remembering every sweet inch of her. "Ah, God!" he breathed when he had her completely naked before him. "You're more beautiful than ever. I've missed you so!"

Gem's eyes twinkled mischievously up at him as she began to undo his tie. "Does that mean this would be a good time to ask you for anything I want?" she asked solemnly.

"Anything at all," he agreed, his eyes darkening with arousal as her fingers brushed his chest while she unbuttoned his shirt. "Whatever it is, I'll get it for you."

"Promise?" she asked innocently, pulling his shirt from his belt, then moving her hands to undo the buckle.

"Promise," he said in an increasingly unsteady voice.

"Well, then," Gem said as she began to tug at the zipper of his trousers, "what I want is for you to let me make mad love to you, the way I did at the cabin at Lake Texhoma, remember?"

"Gem . . ." Roan groaned as he stepped out of his trousers. "Don't you have any self-control at all?" he murmured in mock complaint.

"Uh-uh," she admitted blithely, her tongue between her teeth as she inspected his nude physique admiringly. "I'm one of those undisciplined artists who can't control their basic urges."

She looked up then to see laughter in Roan's dark eyes as he scooped her into his arms and tossed her down onto the bed. "Well, hell, if it's a case of basic urges," he quipped with supreme confidence as he landed beside her, "then I'm your man. I'm loaded with them myself."

"I know," Gem said with a sigh of contented arousal as he pulled her into his arms and molded her against him. "That's one of the things I love about you."

"Just one of the things?" he questioned gently as his mouth began to rove her skin.

"One of many things," Gem admitted happily, shuddering under his touch, coming alive to her senses for the first time in weeks.

"Good," he murmured with deep satisfaction. "Remind me to tell you some of the things I love about you just as soon as I get through satisfying some of these basic urges that drive the two of us so hard."

"No need to hurry," Gem said with an inward gasp as Roan honed in on a *very* basic urge. "We've got all the time in the world to tell each other everything there is to know about our love."

"That's what you think," Roan muttered against her breast. "I hate know-it-alls, too, and I have the feeling we won't get it all said until one or the other of us is not there to listen any longer."

"Ah, but Roan," Gem murmured, her voice slurring with passion, her eyes drugged with wanting, "I promised *never* to leave you, remember?"

"Yes, sweetheart, and I'm going to see that you live up to your promises," Roan whispered raggedly. "Now shut up and let me do something about this basic urge, which is going to kill me if I don't give in to it."

And Gem did, more than happy to save the life of the man she loved, and managing to satisfy quite a few of her own urges in the process.

LOOK FOR NEXT MONTH'S CANDLELIGHT ECSTASY ROMANCES ®

178 A SUMMER'S EMBRACE, *Cathie Linz*
179 DESERT SPLENDOR, *Samantha Hughes*
180 LOST WITHOUT LOVE, *Elizabeth Raffel*
181 A TEMPTING STRANGER, *Lori Copeland*
182 DELICATE BALANCE, *Emily Elliott*
183 A NIGHT TO REMEMBER, *Shirley Hart*
184 DARK SURRENDER, *Diana Blayne*
185 TURN BACK THE DAWN, *Nell Kincaid*

When
You Want
A Little
More Than
Romance—

Try A
Candlelight
Ecstasy!

Wherever paperback
books are sold!

A cold-hearted bargain...
An all-consuming love...

THE TIGER'S WOMAN

by Celeste De Blasis
bestselling author of *The Proud Breed*

Mary Smith made a bargain with Jason Drake, the man they called The Tiger: his protection for her love, his strength to protect her secret. It was a bargain she swore to keep...until she learned what it really meant to be The Tiger's Woman.

A Dell Book $3.95 11820-4

At your local bookstore or use this handy coupon for ordering:

DELL BOOKS THE TIGER'S WOMAN $3.95 (11820-4)
P.O. BOX 1000, PINE BROOK, N.J. 07058-1000

Please send me the above title. I am enclosing $ ________ (please add 75c per copy to cover postage and handling). Send check or money order—no cash or C.O.D.'s. Please allow up to 8 weeks for shipment.

Mr. Mrs./Miss ________________

Address ________________

City ________________ State/Zip ________________